NEW TECHNOLOGIES OF AIR POLLUTION

NEW TECHNOLOGIES OF AIR POLLUTION

By

Prof. (Dr.) Narendra Sharma
Vice Chancellor
Motherhood University
Roorkee (Uttarakhand)
(India)

&

Prof. (Dr.) Abhishek Swami
Professor & Head
Faculty of Science
Motherhood University, Roorkee
Distt- Haridwar (Uttarakhand)
(India)

DISCOVERY PUBLISHING HOUSE PVT. LTD.
INDIA

Published by:

DISCOVERY PUBLISHING HOUSE PVT. LTD.
4383/4B, Ansari Road, Darya Ganj
New Delhi-110 002 (India)
Phone : +91-11-23279245; 23253475; 43596065
E-mail : discoverybooksindia@gmail.com
discoverypublishinghouse@gmail.com
namitwasan9@gmail.com
web : www.discoverypublishinggroup.com

***First Edition:* 2022**

ISBN: 978-93-88854-90-0

New Technologies of Air Pollution

Printed at:
Infinity Imaging Systems
Delhi

Preface

This book has been organized according the syllabi of Environmental Sciences for under graduate and post graduate students of different universities and colleges.

The modern ecology and environment have embraced not only old philosophy of live and let live but the very recent tools and techniques required to establish the causes and consequences of the ongoing changes in the environment, which the human kind never realized earlier.

This textbook giving a basic idea of Control of Air Pollution, Air Pollution from Automobiles, Control of Air Pollution from Automobiles, Dispersion of Air Pollutants, Air Pollution Analysis, Environmental Effects of Air Pollution, Indoor Air Quality and The Air Act.

With the current information on different aspects and problems of Air pollution, we are sure that this edition of the book will be found more useful by all the students who have to study Environmental Science as part of their syllabi for the undergraduate classes.

The authors are highly grateful to all those who have been a source of inspiration, knowledge, and material incorporated in this book. We are sure that the students of undergraduate and post-graduate level will find this book very useful besides those interested in the various aspects of Air polltuion.

The authors are also highly grateful to all the scientists, writers, researchers, and academicians whose work has been cited and or used in different chapters of the book. Finally, we are grateful to the publishers for their interest in publishing the book.

Prof. (Dr.) Narendra Sharma
Prof. (Dr.) Abhishek Swami

Contents

General

The present atmosphere of the earth is probably not its original atmosphere. Our current atmosphere is what chemists would call an *oxidizing atmosphere*, while the original atmosphere was what chemists would call a *reducing atmosphere*. In particular, it probably did not contain oxygen.

Composition of the Atmosphere

The original atmosphere may have been similar to the composition of the solar nebula and close to the present composition of the Gas Giant planets, though this depends on the details of how the planets condensed from the solar nebula. That atmosphere was lost to space, and replaced by compounds out gassed from the crust or (in some more recent theories) much of the atmosphere may have come instead from the impacts of comets and other planetesimals rich in volatile materials.

The oxygen so characteristic of our atmosphere was almost all produced by plants (cyanobacteria or, more colloquially, blue-green algae). Thus, the present composition of the atmosphere is 79% nitrogen, 20% oxygen, and 1% other gases.

Chemical Composition of the Atmosphere

The visible protective thick gaseous cover of air which envelopes the earth is known as atmosphere. It sustains life on earth and saves living organisms from the hostile environment of outer space. It extends to a height of about 1600 km fro earth's surface. The major components of the atmosphere are nitrogen and oxygen while the major components of the atmosphere are nitrogen and oxygen while the minor components are argon, carbon dioxide and some trace gases (in table):

Components	Name of the gas	Per cent by volume
1. Major components	*(i)* Nitrogen	78.09
	(ii) Oxygen	20.94
	(iii) Water vapors	0.1 to 5.0
2. Minor components	*(i)* Argon	9.34×10^{-1}
	(ii) Carbon dioxide	3.25×10^{-2}
3. Trace components	*(i)* Neon	1.82×10^{-3}
	(ii) Helium	5.25×10^{-4}
	(iii) Methane	2×10^{-4}
	(iv) Krypton	1.14×10^{-4}
	(v) Nitrous oxide	2.5×10^{-5}
	(vi) Hydrogen	5×10^{-5}
	(vii) Xenon	8.7×10^{-8}
	(viii) Sulphur dioxide	2×10^{-8}

Atmosphere

It is the transparent gaseous mantle around the earth. It consist of nitrogen (78.03%), oxygen (20.99%), argon (0.94%), carbon dioxide (0.03%), traces of other gases, water vapors, dust particles, etc. Atmosphere has five pats:

(i) **Troposphere:** It extend to about 10-18 km showing fall of temperature with height (15° C to - 55° C), cloud formation, manifestation of weather conditions and presence of dust particles, pollen, spores, etc. in the lower part. Troposphere is sources of gases and medium of locomotion for flying animals.

Modern – day jet planes generally fly through upper part of troposphere and lower part of stratosphere. *Tropopause:* It is transitional layer between troposphere and stratosphere.

(ii) **Stratosphere:** This part of atmosphere occurs between 10-50 km altitude, shows rise of temperature with height (-55° C to-2° C), contains ozone, lacks dust and water vapors. Ozonosphere/Ozone layer: it is part of stratosphere where ozone is concentrated (about 25 km from earth). Ozone layer filters out ultra-violet radiations from solar. *Stratopause:* it is transitional layer between stratosphere and mesosphere.

(iii) **Mesosphere:** The layer extends between 50-85 km from earth's surface and is characterized by decrease in temperature with altitude (-2° C to-92° C). *Mesopause:* it is transitional layer between mesosphere and thermosphere.

(iv) **Thermosphere:** It lies between 85-500 km altitude and shows of temperature with rise of altitude (- 92° C to 1200° C). *Ionosphere:* this layer is a multilayered region of thermosphere which is characterized by presences of ions and free electrons. Ionosphere filters out cosmic and X-rays. Satellites are usually stationed in thermosphere. *Homosphere:* Part of atmosphere upto 100 km altitude which is homogenous in composition due to circulation of movement of air. *Heterospher:* it is outer part of atmosphere or thermosphere which variations in compositions.

(v) **Exosphere:** It is rarefied outer most part of atmosphere (500-1600 km) where particles have tendency to escape into outer space.

Sources of Air Pollution

What is Air Pollution?

Air pollution is the contamination of air by the discharge of harmful substances. Air pollution can cause health problems including burning eyes and nose, itchy irritated throat, and breathing problems. Some chemicals found in polluted air can cause cancer, birth defects, brain and nerve damage, and long-term injury to the lungs and breathing passages in certain circumstances. Above certain concentrations and durations, certain air pollutants are extremely dangerous and can cause severe injury or death.

Air pollution can also damage the environment and property. Trees, lakes, and animals have been harmed by air pollution. Air pollution has thinned the protective ozone layer above the Earth. Air pollution can damage buildings, monuments, statues, and other structures.

Air pollution also can result in haze, which reduces visibility in national parks and elsewhere, and can sometimes interfere with aviation.

What are the Major Air Pollutants?

Carbon Monoxide (CO) is an odorless, colorless gas. After being inhaled, CO molecules can enter the bloodstream, where they inhibit the delivery of oxygen throughout the body. Low concentrations can cause dizziness, headaches, and fatigue; high concentrations can be fatal.

CO is produced by the incomplete burning of carbon-based fuels, including gasoline, oil, and wood. It is also produced from incomplete combustion of natural and synthetic products, such as cigarette smoke. It can build up in high concentrations in enclosed areas such as garages, poorly ventilated tunnels, and even along roadsides in heavy traffic.

Carbon Dioxide (CO_2) is the principal greenhouse gas emitted as a result of human activity (e.g., burning of coal, oil, and natural gas). CO_2 can cause burns, frostbite, and blindness if an area is exposed to it in solid or liquid form. If inhaled, it can be toxic in high concentrations, causing an increase in the breathing rate, unconsciousness, and death.

Hazardous Air Pollutants (HAPs) are chemicals that cause serious health and environmental effects. Health effects include cancer, birth defects, nervous system problems, and death due to massive accidental releases, such as the disaster that occurred at a pesticide plant in Bhopal, India. Hazardous air pollutants are released by sources such as chemical plants, dry cleaners, printing plants, and motor vehicles including cars, trucks, buses, planes.

Lead is a highly toxic metal that produces a range of adverse health effects particularly in young children. Lead can cause nervous system damage and digestive problems, and some lead-containing chemicals cause cancer. Lead can also harm wildlife.

Lead has been phased out of gasoline, which has considerably reduced the contamination of air by lead. However, lead can still be inhaled or ingested from other sources. The sources for lead include paint (for houses and cars), smelters, manufacture of lead batteries, fishing lures, certain parts of bullets, some ceramic ware, miniblinds, water pipes, and a few hair dye products.

Ozone (O_3) is a gas that is a variety of oxygen. Oxygen consists of two oxygen atoms; ozone consists of three. Ozone in the upper atmosphere, where it occurs naturally in what is known as the ozone layer, shields the Earth from the sun's dangerous ultraviolet rays. However, at ground level where it is a pollutant with highly toxic effects, ozone damages human health, the environment, crops, and a wide range of natural and artificial materials. Ground-level ozone can irritate the respiratory tract, cause chest pain, persistent cough, an inability to take a deep breath, and an increased susceptibility to lung infection. Ozone can damage trees and plants and reduce visibility.

Ground-level ozone comes from the breakdown (oxidation) of volatile organic compounds found in solvents. It is also a product of reactions between chemicals that are produced by burning coal, gasoline, other fuels, and chemicals found in paints and hair sprays. Oxidation occurs readily during hot weather. Vehicles and industries are major sources of ground-level ozone.

Nitrogen Oxide (NOx) is a major contributor to smog and acid rain. Nitrogen oxides react with volatile organic compounds to form smog. In high doses, smog can harm humans by causing breathing difficulty for asthmatics, coughs in children, and general illness of the respiratory system. Acid rain can harm vegetation and run into lakes and rivers which changes the chemistry of the water, and makes it potentially uninhabitable for all but acid-tolerant bacteria. Nitrogen oxides are produced from burning fuels, including gasoline and coal. NOx acid aerosols can reduce visibility.

Particulate Matter is any type of solid in the air in the form of smoke, dust, and vapors, which can remain suspended for extended periods. Aside from reducing visibility and soiling clothing, microscopic particles in the air can be breathed into lung tissue becoming lodged and causing increased respiratory disease and lung damage. Particulates are also the main source of haze, which reduces visibility.

Particulates are produced by many sources, including burning of diesel fuels by trucks and buses, fossil fuels, mixing and application of fertilizers and pesticides, road construction, industrial processes such as steel making, mining, agricultural burning, and operation of fireplaces and woodstoves.

Sulfur Dioxide (SO_2) is an odorless gas at low concentrations, but can have a very strong smell at high concentrations. SO_2 is a gas produced by burning coal, most notably in power plants. Some industrial processes, such as production of paper and smelting of metals, produce sulfur dioxide.

Like nitrogen oxides, SO_2 is a major contributor to smog and acid rain. SO_2 is closely related to sulfuric acid, a strong acid. It can harm vegetation and metals and can cause lung problems, including breathing problems and permanent damage to lungs.

Volatile Organic Compounds (VOCs) are organic chemicals. All organic compounds contain carbon, and organic chemicals are the basic chemicals found in all living things and in all products derived from living things. Many organic compounds we use do not occur in nature, but were synthesized by chemists in laboratories. Volatile chemicals produce vapors easily. At room temperature vapors readily escape from volatile liquid chemicals.

VOCs include gasoline, industrial chemicals such as benzene, solvents such as toluene and xylene, and perchloroethylene (principal dry cleaning solvent). VOCs are released from burning fuel, such as gasoline, wood, coal, natural gas and from solvents, paints, glues, and other products used at home or work. Vehicle emissions are an important source of VOCs. Many VOCs are hazardous air pollutants; for example, benzene causes cancer.

Ozone Depletion

Another global concern is depletion of stratospheric ozone. A natural concentration of ozone is found in a sort of "layer" about 19 km above the Earth's surface, in the Earth's upper atmosphere. This protective ozone layer shields the Earth and all living things from lethal ultraviolet (UV) radiation emitted by our sun and thus is essential in making Earth's lands and upper oceans habitable.

Chlorofluorocarbons (CFCs), halons, and other artificial compounds, which were in common use in developed countries for decades as coolants for refrigerators and air conditioners, propellants for aerosol sprays, and other purposes, gradually loft to the upper atmosphere after release. There they act to increase chemical reactions that break down ozone. This allows more UV radiation to reach the Earth's surface, where the UV rays increase the incidence of skin cancer and cataracts and may damage the human immune system as well as harm other animals and plants on land and in the sea.

Most nations are complying with the 1987 Montreal Protocol on Substances that Deplete the Ozone Layer and other international agreements to phase out harmful ozone-depleting chemicals. However, these chemical compounds are very persistent in the environment and continue to cause stratosphere ozone loss. Expert predictions suggest that, if all goes well, thinning of the ozone layer may turn around in about 2008. By around 2045 to 2050, the ozone layer may be restored to its natural equilibratory thickness.

Air pollution is responsible for major health effects. Every year, the health of countless people is ruined or endangered by air pollution.

Many different chemicals in the air affect the human body in negative ways. Just how sick people will get depends on what chemicals they are exposed to, in what concentrations, and for how long.

Studies have estimated that the number of people killed annually in the US alone could be over 50,000.

Older people are highly vulnerable to diseases induced by air pollution. Those with heart or lung disorders are under additional risk. Children and infants are also at serious risk.

Because people are exposed to so many potentially dangerous pollutants, it is often hard to know exactly which pollutants are responsible for causing sickness. Also, because a mixture of different pollutants can intensify sickness, it is often difficult to isolate those pollutants that are at fault.

Many diseases could be caused by air pollution without their becoming apparent for a long time. Diseases such as bronchitis, lung cancer, and heart disease may all eventually appear in people exposed to air pollution.

Air pollutants such as ozone, nitrogen oxides, and sulfur dioxide also have harmful effects on natural ecosystems. They can kill plants and trees by destroying their leaves, and can kill animals, especially fish in highly polluted rivers.

Did you know?

The Industrial Revolution in Europe in the19th Century first saw the beginning of air pollution, which gradually became a major global problem.

The major air-polluting industries are iron, steel and, cement.

Of the 35-40 million tonnes of flyash generated annually by thermal power plants in India, only 2-3 percent is productively utilized.

The worst industrial disaster in India, occurred in 1984 in Bhopal the capital of Madhya Pradesh. A deadly chemical, methly isocyanate leaked out of the Union Carbide factory killing more than 2500 and leaving thousands sick. In fact the effects of this gas tragedy is being felt even today.

Every year some 50 million cars are added to the world's roads. Car making is now the largest manufacturing industry in the world.

In India the number of motorized vehicles have increased from 0.2 million in 1947 to 36.3 million in 1997.

The number of registered vehicles in Delhi is more than the sum total of registered vehicles in Mumbai, Calcutta, and Chennai.

Major contributor to Delhi's air pollution are vehicles.

Nearly three-fourths of India's population, which is rural, bears 84% of the burden of exposure to air pollution.

Growing population, poverty, and inadequate access to clean fuels in rural areas have perpetuated the use of biomass, thereby condemning more than 90% of rural households and more than 35% of urban hoseholds to high levels of indoor air pollution.

One of the most important measure to counter pollution is planting trees. With neem and peepal being the largest emitters of oxygen, planting them in the gardens purifies the surrounding air and helps in maintaining hygienic conditions. While champa, mogra and chameli have better chances of surviving pollution in summer, bulbous varieties do better in winter.

El Nino

El Nino is a shift in ocean temperatures and atmospheric conditions in the tropical Pacific that disrupts weather around the world. It is a poorly understood recurrent climatic phenomenon that primarily affects the Pacific coast of South America, but has dramatic impacts on weather patterns all over the world.

Pronounced 'El-Ninyo', it means 'the boy' in Spanish and was named so by Peruvian fishermen after the Christ child since its effects are generally first felt around Christmas. It is a periodic warming of the Pacific Ocean that leads to terrible extremes of weather. The precise causes, intensity, and longevity of El Nino are not very well understood. The warm El Nino phase typically lasts for 8-10 months or so.

Normally, trade winds blow towards the west, across the Pacific, pushing warm surface water away from the South American coast towards Australia and The Philippines. Along the Peruvian coast the water is cold and nutrient-rich, supporting high levels of primary productivity, diverse marine ecosystems, and major fisheries. During El Nino, the trade winds relax in the central and western Pacific. This allows warm water to accumulate in the surface, which causes the nutrients produced by the upwelling of cold water to significantly come down, leading to the killing of plankton and other aquatic life such as fish and the starvation of many seabirds. This is called the El-Nino effect, which is also responsible for destructive disruptions of worldwide weather patterns.

A wide variety of disasters have been blamed on the El-Nino effect including a famine in Indonesia in 1983, bush fires in Australia arising from droughts, rainstorms in California, and the destruction of anchovy fishery off the coast of Peru. During 1982/83 it is said to have led to the death of some 2000 people worldwide and caused losses amounting to approximately 12 billion dollars.

The impact of the 1997/98 spell of the phenomena was very damaging. Floods devastated the Americas, storms hit China, drought parched Austria, and forest fires burnt parts of South-East Asia and Brazil. Indonesia experienced the worst drought in the last 50 years and in Mexico, the town of Guadalajara saw snow for the first time since 1881. In the Indian Ocean, it affected the movement of the monsoon winds.

When pressure is high in the Pacific Ocean it tends to be low in the Indian Ocean from Africa to Australia. This was the first recognition that changes across the tropical Pacific and beyond were not isolated phenomena but were connected as part of a larger oscillation.

La Nina

This phenomenon generally follows an El Nino. La Nina is sometimes referred to as El Viejo, The Little Girl, anti-El Nino, or simply 'a cold event' or 'a cold episode'. La Nina (pronounced Lah Nee-Nyah) is the cooling of water in the Pacific Ocean.

It is characterized by unusually cold ocean temperatures in the Equatorial Pacific, compared to El Nino, which is characterized by unusually warm ocean temperatures in the Equatorial Pacific. Typically, La Nina occurs roughly half as often as El Nino.

The impacts of La Nina impact on the global climate and ocean temperature tend to be opposite those of El Nino. In the US, winter temperatures are warmer than normal in the south-east and cooler than normal in the north-west during a La Nina year. temperatures are warmer than normal in the Southeast and cooler than normal in the Northwest.

Snow and rain is experienced on the west-coast and unusually cold weather in Alaska. During this period there are higher than normal number of hurricanes in the Atlantic.

El Nino and La Nina are the most powerful phenomenon on the earth and alter the climate across more than half the planet.

Air Pollution Fact Sheet (for New Drivers)

What is Air Pollution?

Air pollution is the contamination of air by the discharge of harmful substances. Air pollution can cause health problems including burning eyes and nose, itchy irritated throat, and breathing problems. Some chemicals found in polluted air can cause cancer, birth defects, brain and nerve damage, and long-term injury to the lungs and breathing passages in certain circumstances. Above certain concentrations and durations, certain air pollutants are extremely dangerous and can cause severe injury or death.

Air pollution can also damage the environment and property. Trees, lakes, and animals have been harmed by air pollution. Air pollution has thinned the protective ozone layer above the Earth. Air pollution can damage buildings, monuments, statues, and other structures.

Air pollution also can result in haze, which reduces visibility in national parks and elsewhere, and can sometimes interfere with aviation.

What Are the Major Air Pollutants?

Carbon Monoxide (CO) is an odorless, colorless gas. After being inhaled, CO molecules can enter the bloodstream, where they inhibit the delivery of oxygen throughout the body. Low concentrations can cause dizziness, headaches, and fatigue; high concentrations can be fatal.

CO is produced by the incomplete burning of carbon-based fuels, including gasoline, oil, and wood. It is also produced from incomplete combustion of natural and synthetic products, such as cigarette smoke. It can build up in high concentrations in enclosed areas such as garages, poorly ventilated tunnels, and even along roadsides in heavy traffic.

Carbon Dioxide (CO_2) is the principal greenhouse gas emitted as a result of human activity (e.g., burning of coal, oil, and natural gas). CO_2 can cause burns, frostbite, and blindness if an area is exposed to it in solid or liquid form. If inhaled, it can be toxic in high concentrations, causing an increase in the breathing rate, unconsciousness, and death.

Chlorofluorocarbons (CFCs) are chemicals used in great quantities in industry, for refrigeration and air conditioning, and in consumer products. CFCs, when released into the air, rise into the stratosphere (a layer of atmosphere high above the Earth). In the stratosphere, CFCs take part in chemical reactions that result in reduction of the stratospheric ozone layer, which protects the Earth's surface from the sun. Reducing the release of CFC emissions and eliminating the production and use of ozone-destroying chemicals is very important to the Earth's stratosphere.

Hazardous Air Pollutants (HAPs) are chemicals that cause serious health and environmental effects. Health effects include cancer, birth defects, nervous system problems, and death due to massive accidental releases, such as the disaster that occurred at a pesticide plant in Bhopal, India.

Hazardous air pollutants are released by sources such as chemical plants, dry cleaners, printing plants, and motor vehicles including cars, trucks, buses, planes.

Lead is a highly toxic metal that produces a range of adverse health effects particularly in young children. Lead can cause nervous system damage and digestive problems, and some lead-containing chemicals cause cancer. Lead can also harm wildlife.

Lead has been phased out of gasoline, which has considerably reduced the contamination of air by lead. However, lead can still be inhaled or ingested from other sources. The sources for lead include paint (for houses and cars), smelters, manufacture of lead batteries, fishing lures, certain parts of bullets, some ceramic ware, miniblinds, water pipes, and a few hair dye products.

Ozone (O_3 is a gas that is a variety of oxygen. Oxygen consists of two oxygen atoms; ozone consists of three. Ozone in the upper atmosphere, where it occurs naturally in what is known as the ozone layer, shields the Earth from the sun's dangerous ultraviolet rays. However, at ground level where it is a pollutant with highly toxic effects, ozone damages human health, the environment, crops, and a wide range of natural and artificial materials. Ground-level ozone can irritate the respiratory tract, cause chest pain, persistent cough, an inability to take a deep breath, and an increased susceptibility to lung infection. Ozone can damage trees and plants and reduce visibility.

Ground-level ozone comes from the breakdown (oxidation) of volatile organic compounds found in solvents. It is also a product of reactions between chemicals that are produced by burning coal, gasoline, other fuels, and chemicals found in paints and hair sprays. Oxidation occurs readily during hot weather. Vehicles and industries are major sources of ground-level ozone.

Nitrogen Oxide (NO_x) is a major contributor to smog and acid rain. Nitrogen oxides react with volatile organic compounds to form smog. In high doses, smog can harm humans by causing breathing difficulty for asthmatics, coughs in children, and general illness of the respiratory system. Acid rain can harm vegetation and run into lakes and rivers which changes the chemistry of the water, and makes it potentially uninhabitable for all but acid-tolerant bacteria.

Nitrogen oxides are produced from burning fuels, including gasoline and coal. (NO_x) acid aerosols can reduce visibility.

Particulate Matter is any type of solid in the air in the form of smoke, dust, and vapors, which can remain suspended for extended periods. Aside from reducing visibility and soiling clothing, microscopic particles in the air can be breathed into lung tissue becoming lodged and causing increased respiratory disease and lung damage. Particulates are also the main source of haze, which reduces visibility.

Particulates are produced by many sources, including burning of diesel fuels by trucks and buses, fossil fuels, mixing and application of fertilizers and pesticides, road construction, industrial processes such as steel making, mining, agricultural burning, and operation of fireplaces and woodstoves.

Sulfur Dioxide (SO_2) is an odorless gas at low concentrations, but can have a very strong smell at high concentrations. SO_2 is a gas produced by burning coal, most notably in power plants. Some industrial processes, such as production of paper and smelting of metals, produce sulfur dioxide.

Like nitrogen oxides, SO_2 is a major contributor to smog and acid rain. SO_2 is closely related to sulfuric acid, a strong acid. It can harm vegetation and metals and can cause lung problems, including breathing problems and permanent damage to lungs.

Volatile Organic Compounds (VOCs) are organic chemicals. All organic compounds contain carbon, and organic chemicals are the basic chemicals found in all living things and in all products derived from living things. Many organic compounds we use do not occur in nature, but were synthesized by chemists in laboratories. Volatile chemicals produce vapors easily. At room temperature vapors readily escape from volatile liquid chemicals.

VOCs include gasoline, industrial chemicals such as benzene, solvents such as toluene and xylene, and perchloroethylene (principal dry cleaning solvent). VOCs are released from burning fuel, such as gasoline, wood, coal, natural gas and from solvents, paints, glues, and other products used at home or work. Vehicle emissions are an important source of VOCs. Many VOCs are hazardous air pollutants; for example, benzene causes cancer.

How can I reduce my contribution to air pollution?

There are many ways to reduce air pollution. People can contribute significantly to cleaning the air if they take (or do not take — as the case may be) certain simple actions to reduce air pollution.

Since vehicles contribute greatly to air pollution by emitting CO, NO_x, ozone, VOCs, HAPs, CFCs, and particulate matter, each driver who makes personal changes in driving habits contributes to the reduction of air pollution.

Limit driving, use public transportation, walk, use carpools, bike, or so forth. These are the best ways an individual can help reduce air pollution!

If you must drive, then try to follow these guidelines:

- Avoid high speeds.
- Buy a vehicle with high miles per gallon.
- Do not overfill or top off your gasoline tank.
- Do not refuel on high ozone days — try to refuel after dark.
- Drive a newer vehicle; the new models generally pollute less.
- Drive alternative vehicles or alternatively fueled vehicles, such as electric vehicles.
- Drive smoothly and avoid lengthy idling.
- If the vehicle is a pre-1995 model, have a professional convert the air conditioning from the dangerous CFC R-12 to the safer R-134a to reduce your contribution to the ozone hole.
- Keep your car well maintained, especially the emissions control system.

- Keep tires properly inflated.
- Maintain your vehicle's air conditioning system — do not allow it to leak.
- Make fewer trips in your vehicle — plan routes to avoid traffic.
- Reduce fuel use as often as possible — a vehicle's shape and design features can affect its fuel use.

Here are other actions individuals can take to reduce air pollution:

- Defer lawn and gardening chores that use gasoline-powered equipment on high ground-level ozone days.
- Eat organically grown food, or at least less pesticide-dependant foods.
- Limit dry cleaning.
- Postpone using oil-based paint and solvents on high ground-level ozone days.
- Reduce consumption of electricity — conserving reduces emissions of SO_2, NO_x, VOCs and particulate matter into the air.
- Start charcoal with an electric or chimney-type fire starter instead of lighter fluid.
- Reduce, Reuse, Recycle — less consumption of products will reduce all types of air pollution!

Air pollution can affect our health in many ways with both *short-term* and *long-term* effects. Different groups of individuals are affected by air pollution in different ways. Some individuals are much more sensitive to pollutants than are others. Young children and elderly people often suffer more from the effects of air pollution. People with health problems such as asthma, heart and lung disease may also suffer more when the air is polluted. The extent to which an individual is harmed by air pollution usually depends on the total exposure to the damaging chemicals, i.e., the *duration of exposure* and the *concentration of the chemicals* must be taken into account.

Examples of short-term effects include irritation to the eyes, nose and throat, and upper respiratory infections such as bronchitis and pneumonia. Other symptoms can include headaches, nausea, and allergic reactions. Short-term air pollution can aggravate the medical conditions of individuals with asthma and emphysema. In the great "Smog Disaster" in London in 1952, four thousand people died in a few days due to the high concentrations of pollution.

Long-term health effects can include chronic respiratory disease, lung cancer, heart disease, and even damage to the brain, nerves, liver, or kidneys. Continual exposure to air pollution affects the lungs of growing children and may aggravate or complicate medical conditions in the elderly. It is estimated that half a million people die prematurely every year in the United States as a result of smoking cigarettes.

Research into the health effects of air pollution is ongoing. Medical conditions arising from air pollution can be very expensive. Healthcare costs, lost productivity in the workplace, and human welfare impacts cost billions of dollars each year.

Air and its major Pollutants

One of the formal definitions of air pollution is as follows – 'The presence in the atmosphere of one or more contaminants in such quality and for such duration as is injurious, or tends to be injurious, to human health or welfare, animal or plant life.' It is the contamination of air by the discharge of harmful substances. Air pollution can cause health problems and it can also damage the environment and property. It has caused thinning of the protective ozone layer of the atmosphere, which is leading to climate change.

Modernisation and progress have led to air getting more and more polluted over the years. Industries, vehicles, increase in the population, and urbanization are some of the major factors responsible for air pollution. The following industries are among those that emit a great deal of pollutants into the air: thermal power plants, cement, steel, refineries, petro chemicals, and mines.

Air pollution results from a variety of causes, not all of which are within human control. Dust storms in desert areas and smoke from forest fires and grass fires contribute to chemical and particulate pollution of the air. The source of pollution may be in one country but the impact of pollution may be felt elsewhere. The discovery of pesticides in Antarctica, where they have never been used, suggests the extent to which aerial transport can carry pollutants from one place to another. Probably the most important natural source of air pollution is volcanic activity, which at times pours great amounts of ash and toxic fumes into the atmosphere. The eruptions of such volcanoes as Krakatoa in Indonesia, Mt. St. Helens in Washington, USA and Katmai in Alaska, USA, have been related to measurable climatic changes.

National Ambient Air Quality Standards

Pollutants	Average Time	Concentration
Sulphur dioxide (SO_2)	Annual average	60 μg/m^3
	24 hour	80 μg/m^3
Oxides of Nitrogen (NO_2)	A.A	60 μg/m^3
	24H	80 μg/m^3
Suspended Particulate Matter (SPM)	A.A	140 μg/m^3
	24H	200 μg/m^3
Lead	A.A	0.75 μg/m^3
	24H	1.0 μg/m^3
Carbon Monoxide	A.A	2.0 μg/m^3
	24H	4.0 μg/m^3
Respirable Particulate Matter (RPM)	A.A	60 μg/m^3
	24H	100 μg/m^3

Listed below are the major air pollutants and their sources.

Carbon monoxide (CO) is a colourless, odourless gas that is produced by the incomplete burning of carbon-based fuels including petrol, diesel, and wood. It is also produced from the combustion of natural and synthetic products such as cigarettes. It lowers the amount of oxygen that enters our blood. It can slow our reflexes and make us confused and sleepy.

Carbon dioxide (CO_2) is the principle greenhouse gas emitted as a result of human activities such as the burning of coal, oil, and natural gases.

Chloroflorocarbons (CFC) are gases that are released mainly from air-conditioning systems and refrigeration. When released into the air, CFCs rise to the stratosphere, where they come in contact with few other gases, which leads to a reduction of the ozone layer that protects the earth from the harmful ultraviolet rays of the sun.

Lead is present in petrol, diesel, lead batteries, paints, hair dye products, etc. Lead affects children in particular. It can cause nervous system damage and digestive problems and, in some cases, cause cancer.

Ozone occur naturally in the upper layers of the atmosphere. This important gas shields the earth from the harmful ultraviolet rays of the sun. However, at the ground level, it is a pollutant with highly toxic effects. Vehicles and industries are the major source of ground-level ozone emissions. Ozone makes our eyes itch, burn, and water. It lowers our resistance to colds and pneumonia.

Nitrogen oxide (Nox) causes smog and acid rain. It is produced from burning fuels including petrol, diesel, and coal. Nitrogen oxides can make children susceptible to respiratory diseases in winters.

Suspended particulate matter (SPM) consists of solids in the air in the form of smoke, dust, and vapour that can remain suspended for extended periods and is also the main source of haze which reduces visibility. The finer of these particles, when breathed in can lodge in our lungs and cause lung damage and respiratory problems.

Sulphur dioxide (SO_2) is a gas produced from burning coal, mainly in thermal power plants. Some industrial processes, such as production of paper and smelting of metals, produce sulphur dioxide. It is a major contributor to smog and acid rain. Sulfur dioxide can lead to lung diseases.

Effects of Air Pollution

The Effect of Air Pollution on Plants

The burning of hydrocarbons in motor vehicle engines gives rise to CO_2, CO, SO_2 (sulfur dioxide), NO_x (NO [nitrogen monoxide]) and NO_2^- in varying proportions), and C_2H_4 (ethylene), as well as a variety of other hydrocarbons. Additional SO_2 originates from domestic and industrial burning of fossil fuels. Industrial plants, such as chemical works and metal-smelting plants, release SO_2, H_2S, NO_2, and HF (hydrogen fluoride) into the atmosphere. Tall chimney stacks may be used to carry gases and particles to a high altitude and thus avoid local pollution, but the pollutants return to Earth, sometimes hundreds of kilometers from the original source.

Photochemical smog is the product of chemical reactions driven by sunlight and involving NO_x of urban and industrial origin and volatile organic compounds from either vegetation (*biogenic* hydrocarbons) or human activities (*anthropogenic* hydrocarbons). Ozone (O_3) and peroxyacetylnitrate (PAN) produced in these complex reactions can become injurious to plants and other life forms, depending on concentration and duration of exposure. Hydrogen peroxide, another potentially injurious molecule, can form by the reaction between O_3 and naturally released volatiles (terpenes) from forest trees.

The concentrations of polluting gases, or their solutions, to which plants are exposed are thus highly variable, depending on location, wind direction, rainfall, and sunlight. In urban areas, concentrations of SO_2 and NO_x in air are typically 0.02 to 0.5 mL L^{-1}, the upper value being within the range that is inhibitory to plant growth. Relatively long-term experiments at appropriate concentrations of pollutants are necessary to establish the real impact of air pollution on vegetation. The reaction of plants to high concentrations of pollutants in short-term experiments may overwhelm the plant's defense mechanisms and provoke abnormal symptoms.

The responses of plants to polluting gases can also be affected by other ambient conditions, such as light, humidity, temperature, and the supply of water and minerals. Experiments aimed at determining the impact of chronic exposure to low concentrations of gases should allow plants to grow under near-natural conditions. One method is to grow the plants in open-top chambers into which gases are carefully metered, or where plants receiving ambient, polluted air are compared with controls receiving air that has been scrubbed of pollutants.

Polluting Gases and Dust Inhibit Stomatal Movements, Photosynthesis, and Growth

Dust pollution is of localized importance near roads, quarries, cement works, and other industrial areas. Apart from screening out sunlight, dust on leaves blocks stomata and lowers their conductance to CO_2, simultaneously interfering with photosystem II. Polluting gases such as SO_2 and NO_x enter leaves through stomata, following the same diffusion pathway as CO_2. NO_x dissolves in cells and gives rise to nitrite ions (NO_2^-, which are toxic at high concentrations) and nitrate ions (NO_3^-) that enter into nitrogen metabolism as if they had been absorbed through the roots. In some cases, exposure to pollutant gases, particularly SO_2, causes stomatal closure, which protects the leaf against further entry of the pollutant but also curtails photosynthesis. In the cells, SO_2 dissolves to give bisulfite and sulfite ions; sulfite is toxic, but at low concentrations it is metabolized by chloroplasts to sulfate, which is not toxic. At sufficiently low concentrations, bisulfite and sulfite are effectively detoxified by plants, and SO_2 air pollution then provides a sulfur source for the plant.

In urban areas these polluting gases may be present in such high concentrations that they cannot be detoxified rapidly enough to avoid injury. Ozone is presently considered to be the most damaging phytotoxic air pollutant in North America (Heagle 1989; Krupa *et al.*, 1995). It has been estimated that wherever the mean daily O_3 concentration reaches 40, 50, or 60 ppb (parts per billion, or per 10^9), the combined yields of soybean, maize, winter wheat, and cotton would be decreased by 5, 10, and 16%, respectively.

Ozone is highly reactive: It binds to plasma membranes and it alters metabolism. As a result, stomatal apertures are poorly regulated, chloroplast thylakoid membranes are damaged, rubisco is degraded, and photosynthesis is inhibited. Ozone reacts with O_2 and produces reactive oxygen species, including hydrogen peroxide (H_2O_2), superoxide (O_2^-), singlet oxygen ($^1O_2^*$), and the hydroxyl radical (•OH). These denature proteins, damage nucleic acids and thereby give rise to mutations, and cause lipid peroxidation, which breaks down lipids in membranes. Reactive oxygen species form also in the absence of O_3, particularly in electron transport in the mitochondria and chloroplasts, when electrons can be donated to O_2.

Cells are protected, at least in part, from reactive oxygen species by enzymatic and nonenzymatic defense mechanisms (Bowler *et al.*, 1992; Elstner and Osswald 1994). Defense against reactive oxygen species is pro vided by the scavenging properties of molecules such as ascorbic acid, α-tocopherol, phenolic compounds, and glutathione. Superoxide dismutases (SODs) catalyze the reduction of superoxide to hydrogen peroxide. Hydrogen peroxide is then converted to H_2O by the action of catalases and peroxidases. Of particular importance is the ascorbate-specific peroxidase localized in the chloroplast. Acting in concert, ascorbate peroxidase, dehydroascorbate reductase, and glutathione reductase remove H_2O_2 in a series of reactions called the *Halliwell–Asada pathway,* named after its discoverers. Glutathione is a sulfur-containing tripeptide that, in its reduced form, reacts rapidly with dehydroascorbate and becomes oxidized in the process. Glutathione reductase catalyzes the regeneration of reduced glutathione (GSH) from its oxidized form (GSSG) in the following reaction:

$$GSSG + NADPH + H^+ \rightarrow 2\ GSH + NADP^+$$

Exposure of plants to reactive oxygen species stimulates the transcription and translation of genes that encode enzymes involved in protection mechanisms. In *Arabidopsis,* exposure for 6 hours per day to low levels of O_3 induces the expression of several genes that encode enzymes associated with protection from reactive oxygen species, including SOD, glutathione S-transferase (which catalyzes detoxification reactions involving glutathione), and phenylalanine ammonia lyase (an important enzyme at the start of the phenylpropanoid pathway leading to the synthesis of flavonoids and other phenolics). In transgenic tobacco transformed with a gene from *Escherichia coli* to give additional glutathione reductase activity in the chloroplast, short-term exposure to high levels of SO_2 is much less damaging than for wild-type tobacco (Aono *et al.*, 1993).

Environmental extremes may either accelerate the production of reactive oxygen species or impair the normal defense mechanisms that protect cells from reactive oxygen species. In water-deficient leaves, for example, greater oxygen photoreduction by photosystems I and II increases superoxide production, and the pool of glutathione, as well as the activity of glutathione reductase, increase, presumably as part of the cell defense mechanism. In contrast, levels of ascorbate, another antioxidant, generally decline with mild water stress. Transgenic plants overexpressing mitochondrion superoxide dismutase (Mn-SOD), the isozyme localized in the mitochondrial matrix, show less water deficit damage and, significantly, improved survival and yield under field conditions (McKersie *et al.*, 1996). In other experiments, transgenic alfalfa overexpressing Mn-SOD, was found to be more tolerant of freezing. Conversely, winter rye, wheat, and barley acclimated at 2° C for several weeks were found to have developed resistance to the herbicides paraquat and acifluorfen, which generate reactive oxygen species. Such investigations support the hypothesis that tolerance of oxidative stress is an important factor in tolerance to a wide range of environmental extremes.

Many deleterious changes in metabolism caused by air pollution precede external symptoms of injury, which appear only at much higher concentrations. For example, when plants are exposed to air containing NO_x, lesions on leaves appear at an NO_x concentration of 5 mL L^{-1}, but photosynthesis starts to be inhibited at a concentration of only 0.1 mL L^{-1}. These low, threshold concentrations refer to the effects of a single pollutant. However, two or more pollutants acting together can have a synergistic effect, producing damage at lower concentrations than if they were acting separately. In addition, vegetation weakened by air pollution can become more susceptible to invasion by pathogens and pests.

Polluting Gases, Dissolved in Rainwater, fall as "Acid Rain"

Unpolluted rain is slightly acidic, with a pH close to 5.6, because the CO_2 dissolved in it produces the weak acid H_2CO_3. Dissolution of NO_x and SO_2 in water droplets in the atmosphere causes the pH of rain to decrease to 3 to 4, and in southern California polluted droplets in fog can be as acidic as pH 1.7. Dilute acidic solution can remove mineral nutrients from leaves, depending on the age of the leaf and the integrity of the cuticle and surface waxes. The total annual contributions to the soil of acid from acid rain (*wet deposition*) and from particulate matter falling on the soil plus direct absorption from the atmosphere (*dry deposition*) may reach 1.0 to 3.0 kg H^+ per hectare in parts of Europe and the northeastern United States (Schwartz 1989). In soils that lack free calcium carbonate, and therefore are not strongly buffered, such additions of acid can be harmful to plants. Furthermore, the added acid can result in the release of aluminum ions from soil minerals, causing aluminum toxicity. Air pollution is considered to be a major factor in the decline of forests in heavily polluted areas of Europe and North America. There are indications that fast-growing pioneer species are better able to tolerate an acidifying atmosphere than are climax forest trees, possibly because they have a greater potential for assimilation of dissolved NO_x, and more effective acid buffering of the leaf tissue cell sap.

Air Pollution Affects Local Trees and Shrubs

The brown cloud, so prevalent in Denver during the fall, may cause injury to trees and shrubs. Researchers at universities in smog-prone areas have studied and documented air pollution damage to plants. These areas include the San Gabriel and the San Bernadino mountains of Southern California. Los Angeles smog drifts eastward into the mountains where it damages pine trees.

Symptoms include browning on needles that occurs in a mottled pattern. Plant specialists call this chlorosis. The browning progresses to premature needle drop, and eventually causes premature death in Ponderosa pines. In the meanwhile, the trees are more susceptible to disease and bark beetle attacks.

Extensive air pollution studies also have been undertaken in the Blue Ridge Mountains of Virginia. Eastern white pines have developed chlorotic spotting and premature needle drop.

Much of the Denver area's air pollution comes from automobile exhaust. Sunlight in the presence of exhaust promotes the formation of a gas called ozone that injures plants.

Symptoms of ozone damage to plants range from slow growth to severe leaf browning, followed by premature leaf drop. On pines, the most frequent symptom is an unusual mottled pattern along the needles. In severe cases, tips turn brown and older needles fall off. Deciduous trees that lose leaves in the fall exhibit a stippling or flecked pattern on the upper leaf surface. Flecks can be white, tan or black depending on the plant species.

Nationally, air pollution injury has been documented on white ash, aspen, Ohio buckeye, Kentucky coffee, Crimean linden, imperial honeylocust, weeping willow and hybrid poplar trees. Other studies have found green ash, silver maple, eastern cottonwood, loblollypine and sycamore trees sensitive to air pollution.

The most likely time to find ozone injury symptoms in the Denver Metro area would be in the fall season. Trees such as linden, maple and green ash may exhibit ozone-injury symptoms. Outer margins of linden tree leaves display a minor black mottling in early August that progresses to severe marginal tissue distruction. Young leaves on maple trees display white flecks much like freckles. Green ash trees lose leaves prematurely and look rather sickly. At Cornell University, researchers have linked ash tree decline to stress from excessive air pollution. How much injury we have in the Denver Metro area is an open question as, at this writing, there is no active research program or expertise on air pollution and plants in Colorado.

Diagnosis from symptoms is difficult because fungal diseases may cause leaf symptoms that mimic air pollution. Local aspen trees have displayed problems that look similar to fungal leaf spots, particularly those of the fungus Marssonina. Colorado State University pathologists, however, have at times been unable to culture Marssonina fungus from aspen samples submitted. This suggests that local aspen trees could be exhibiting ozone damage, not fungal infection.

Local pines and blue spruce may also show signs of air pollution damage. In ozone injury, blue spruce needles are mottled and over-all tree growth is slower than normal. Evergreen trees stressed by ozone and other injuries can become more susceptible to bark beetle infestations and display needle mottling and loss.

Knowing precisely if a tree is suffering from air pollution damage is difficult. Trees of the same species (though of different genetics) growing in identical locations may vary in susceptibility to injury. One tree may show no sign of the problem, while the tree next to it will drop brown needles and die back. It's difficult for tree care professionals to make an accurate diagnosis under these circumstances.

Any injury locally is most likely to be seen from August-October. Older leaves would be the most likely to show symptoms, because they've been exposed to pollutants for longer periods. Fortunately most plants, even those sensitive to damage, are thought to be tolerant of air pollution injury during dormancy. This means that when Denver's brown cloud gets thick in winter, deciduous trees and shrubs that drop their leaves won't suffer further injury.

Note that overall, other causes of stress and injury to plants such as environmental stress (from drought, cold, etc.) and soil conditions (tight clay soils, shallow soils, etc.) are common and the more identifiable causes of Colorado plant growth problems.

Health Impacts of Air Pollution

Since the onset of the industrial revolution, there has been a steady change in the composition of the atmosphere mainly due to the combustion of fossil fuels used for the generation of energy and transportation.

Air pollution is a major environmental health problem affecting the developing and the developed countries alike. The effects of air pollution on health are very complex as there are many different sources and their individual effects vary from one to the other. It is not only the ambient air quality in the cities but also the indoor air quality in the rural and the urban areas that are causing concern. In fact in the developing world the highest air pollution exposures occur in the indoor environment. Air pollutants that are inhaled have serious impact on human health affecting the lungs and the respiratory system; they are also taken up by the blood and pumped all round the body. These pollutants are also deposited on soil, plants, and in the water, further contributing to human exposure. As you read on you can learn about health impacts of specific air pollutants.

Common Atmospheric Pollution Sources and their Pollutants

Category	Source	Emitting pollutants
Agriculture	Open burning	Suspended particulate matter, carbon monoxide, volatile organic compounds
Mining and quarrying	Coal mining; crude oil and gas production; stone quarrying	Suspended particulate matter, sulphur dioxide, oxides of nitrogen, volatile organic compounds
Power generation	Electricity; gas; steam	Suspended particulate matter, sulphur dioxide, oxides of nitrogen, carbon monoxide, volatile organic compounds, sulphur trioxide, lead
Transport	Combustion engines	Suspended particulate matter, sulphur dioxide, oxides of nitrogen, carbon monoxide, volatile organic compounds, lead
Community service	Municipal incinerators	Suspended particulate matter, sulphur dioxide, oxides of nitrogen, carbon monoxide, volatile organic compounds, lead

Impact of Air Pollution on Health

The magnitude of the London fog of 1952, which affected such a large number of people, was the first incident that made people aware of the damage done to the atmosphere due to industrialization. The SPM levels increased manifold and resulted in over 4000 deaths.

Indoor air pollution can be particularly hazardous to health as it is released in close proximity to people. It is stated that a pollutant released indoors is many times more likely to reach the lung than that released outdoors. In the developing countries a fairly large portion of the population is dependent on biomass for their energy requirements. These include wood, charcoal, agricultural residue, and animal waste. Open fires used for cooking and heating are commonly found in the household both in the rural and the urban areas. The stove is often at floor level, adding to the risk of accident and the hygiene factor. In addition, they are often not fitted with a chimney to remove the pollutants. In such households the children and women are most likely to be affected, as they are the group that spends more time indoors. The main pollutant in this environment is the SPM. In fact, death due to indoor air pollution, mainly particulate matters, in the rural areas of India are one of the highest in the world. Many of the deaths are due to acute respiratory infections in children; others are due to cardiovascular diseases, lung cancer, and chronic respiratory diseases in adults. If emissions are high and ventilation is poor, household use of coal and biomass can severely affect the indoor air quality.

Pollutant emissions per meal are also very high compared to those of other fuels. Household use of fossil fuel is also fairly common in the developing countries, particularly coal—both bituminous and lignite. These are particularly damaging as they burn inefficiently and emit considerable quantities of air pollutants. If emissions are high and ventilation poor, then the exposure levels to the gases emitted are far higher. The most harmful of the gases and agents that are emitted are particulate matter, carbon dioxide, polycyclic organic matter, and formaldehyde. The indoor concentrations of these are far higher than the acceptable levels and is cause for concern in rural areas.

Health Impact of Specific Air Pollutants

Some of these gases can seriously and adversely affect the health of the population and should be given due attention by the concerned authority. The gases mentioned below are mainly outdoor air pollutants but some of them can and do occur indoor depending on the source and the circumstances.

- *Tobacco smoke*. Tobacco smoke generates a wide range of harmful chemicals and is a major cause of ill health, as it is known to cause cancer, not only to the smoker but affecting passive smokers too. It is well-known that smoking affects the passive smoker (the person who is in the vicinity of a smoker and is not himself/herself a smoker) ranging from burning sensation in the eyes or nose, and throat irritation, to cancer, bronchitis, severe asthma, and a decrease in lung function.
- *Biological pollutants*. These are mostly allergens that can cause asthma, hay fever, and other allergic diseases.
- *Volatile organic compounds*. Volatile compounds can cause irritation of the eye, nose and throat. In severe cases there may be headaches, nausea, and loss of coordination. In the longer run, some of them are suspected to cause damage to the liver and other parts of the body.
- *Formaldehyde*. Exposure causes irritation to the eyes, nose and may cause allergies in some people.
- *Lead*. Prolonged exposure can cause damage to the nervous system, digestive problems, and in some cases cause cancer. It is especially hazardous to small children.
- *Radon*. A radioactive gas that can accumulate inside the house, it originates from the rocks and soil under the house and its level is dominated by the outdoor air and also to some extent the other gases being emitted indoors. Exposure to this gas increases the risk of lung cancer.
- *Ozone*. Exposure to this gas makes our eyes itch, burn, and water and it has also been associated with increase in respiratory disorders such as asthma. It lowers our resistance to colds and pneumonia.
- *Oxides of nitrogen*. This gas can make children susceptible to respiratory diseases in the winters.
- *Carbon monoxide*. CO (carbon monoxide) combines with haemoglobin to lessen the amount of oxygen that enters our blood through our lungs. The binding with other haeme proteins causes changes in the function of the

affected organs such as the brain and the cardiovascular system, and also the developing foetus. It can impair our concentration, slow our reflexes, and make us confused and sleepy.

- *Sulphur dioxide.* SO_2 (sulphur dioxide) in the air is caused due to the rise in combustion of fossil fuels. It can oxidize and form sulphuric acid mist. SO_2 in the air leads to diseases of the lung and other lung disorders such as wheezing and shortness of breath. Long-term effects are more difficult to ascertain as SO_2 exposure is often combined with that of SPM.
- *SPM (suspended particulate matter).* Suspended matter consists of dust, fumes, mist and smoke. The main chemical component of SPM that is of major concern is lead, others being nickel, arsenic, and those present in diesel exhaust. These particles when breathed in, lodge in our lung tissues and cause lung damage and respiratory problems. The importance of SPM as a major pollutant needs special emphasis as (a) it affects more people globally than any other pollutant on a continuing basis; (b) there is more monitoring data available on this than any other pollutant; and (c) more epidemiological evidence has been collected on the exposure to this than to any other pollutant.

Impact of Air Pollution

Due to the far reaching impact of air pollution on the environment, and in turn the ecological status, it is a key concern.

Plants are more sensitive than humans and animals to the effects of air pollution. The three most important pollutants are ozone (O_3), sulphur dioxide (SO_2) and nitrogen dioxide (NO_2), with a greater impact on annual crops than perennial crops. The Gauteng State of the Environment Report (1995) highlighted the most significant air quality issues as follows:

- Global warming due to the generation of greenhouse gases such as carbon dioxide, ozone and methane.

Air Pollution in Relation to Impact

Pollutant	Source	Health
Ozone (O_3)	Action of sunlight on NO_2, HC's	Asthma; Bronchitis; Irritation to the eyes and mucous membranes; Headaches; Nose & throat irritation
Lead	Transportation Industry	Reduced birth weight and lowered intelligence
Carbon dioxide	Burning of fossil fuels Combustion in motor vehicles	Headaches; Asphyxiation; Impairment of performance on tasks requiring attention; Aggravation of cardiovascular disease; Enhances global warming
Suspended particles	Burning of fossil fuels, untarred roads, mining dust and agriculture	Damage to lung tissues causing respiratory disease
Sulphur dioxide	Burning of fossil fuels (coal)	Causes constriction of the airways in people with asthma, repeated exposure causes a condition similar to bronchitis. Increased risk of acute respiratory disease; Causes acid rain
Nitrogen dioxide	Burning of fossil fuels especially motor vehicles	Can irritate the lungs, aggravate the condition of people suffering from asthma or chronic bronchitis
Hydrocarbons	Vehicles and inudstrial processes	Can cause some defects in babies during pregnancy or cancer. Precursor to photochemical smog, which causes respiratory diseases
Carbon monoxide	Vehicle emissions	Restricts oxygen uptake Causes drowsiness, headaches, death
Heavy metals	Industry and motor vehicles	Health Heavy metals can cause cancer, defects in babies during pregnancy; Lead – Neurocognitive and neuromotor impairment

- Acid deposition where sulphates and nitrates in the atmosphere are deposited in rain, mist or through dry deposition. Acid deposition can lead to the salination and acidification of water resources and of soil.
- Salination of water resources is caused by the accumulation of sulphates and nitrates on the land surface, and their transport into dams and lakes.
- Sulphates and nitrates can increase soil acidity. Concentrations of toxic metals in the soil solution may increase which can impact on plant growth.

Impacts of Air Pollution and Acid Rain on Vegetation

Introduction

"Acid rain" is a general name for many phenomena including acid fog, acid sleet, and acid snow. Although we associate the acid threat with rainy days, acid deposition occurs all the time, even on sunny days.

Sulphur dioxide and nitrogen oxides both combine with water in the atmosphere to create acid rain. Acid rain acidifies the soils and waters where it falls, killing off plants. Many industrial processes produce large quantities of pollutants including sulphur dioxide and nitrous oxide. These are also produced by car engines and are emitted in the exhaust. When sulphur dioxide and nitrous oxide react with water vapour in the atmosphere, acids are produced. The result is what is termed acid rain, which causes serious damage to plants.

In addition, other gaseous pollutants, such as ozone and nitrous oxides, can also harm vegetation directly.

How Acid Rain Harms Trees

Acid rain does not usually kill trees directly. Instead, it is more likely to weaken the trees by damaging their leaves, limiting the nutrients available to them, or poisoning them with toxic substances slowly released from the soil. The main atmospheric pollutants that affect trees are nitrates and sulphates. Forest decline is often the first sign that trees are in trouble due to air pollution.

Scientists believe that acidic water dissolves the nutrients and helpful minerals in the soil and then washes them away before the trees and other plants can use them to grow. At the same time, the acid rain causes the release of toxic substances such as aluminium into the soil. These are very harmful to trees and plants, even if contact is limited. Toxic substances also wash away in the runoff that carries the substances into streams, rivers, and lakes. Fewer of these toxic substances are released when the rainfall is cleaner.

Even if the soil is well buffered, there can be damage from acid rain. Forests in high mountain regions receive additional acid from the acidic clouds and fog that often surround them. These clouds and fog are often more acidic than rainfall. When leaves are frequently bathed in this acid fog, their protective waxy coating can wear away. The loss of the coating damages the leaves and creates brown spots. Leaves turn the energy in sunlight into food for growth. This process is called photosynthesis. When leaves are damaged, they cannot produce enough food energy for the tree to remain healthy.

Once trees are weak, diseases or insects that ultimately kill them can more easily attack them. Weakened trees may also become injured more easily by cold weather.

How Air Pollution Harms Trees

Whilst acid rain is a major cause of damage to vegetation, the air pollutants which are often the precursors to acid rain can also be harmful directly. These include sulphur dioxide, ozone and nitrous oxides.

Sulphur Dioxide

Sulphur dioxide, one of the main components of acid rain, has direct effects on vegetation. Changes in the physical appearance of vegetation are an indication that the plants' metabolism is impaired by the concentration of sulphur dioxide. Harm caused by sulphur dioxide is first noticeable on the leaves of the plants. For some plants injury can occur within hours or days of being exposed to high levels of sulphur dioxide. It is the leaves in mid-growth that are the most vulnerable, while the older and younger leaves are more resistant. You can see the damage to coniferous needles by observing the extreme colour difference between the green base and the bright orange-red tips.

The effects of sulphur dioxide are influenced by other biological and environmental factors such as plant type, age, sunlight levels, temperature, humidity and the presence of other pollutants (ozone and nitrogen oxides). Thus, even though sulphur dioxide levels may be extremely high, the levels may not affect vegetation because of the surrounding environmental conditions. It is also possible that the plants and soils may temporarily store pollutants. By storing the pollutants they are preventing the pollutants from reacting with other substances in the plants or soil.

Ozone

The effects of ozone on plants have been investigated intensively for almost two decades. Studies made in controlled environment (CE) chambers, glasshouse and in the field, using open-topped chambers, have all contributed to the understanding of the mechanisms underlying ozone effects and their ultimate impact on vegetation. The biochemical mechanisms by which ozone interacts with plants have been intensively studied and, although the relative significance of different initial reactions remains unclear, there is a consensus that the key event in plant responses is oxidative damage to cell membranes. This primary oxidative damage results in the loss of membrane integrity and function, and in turn to inhibition of essential biochemical and physiological processes. A key target is photosynthesis, although ozone may also affect stomatal function and so modify plant responses to other factors, such as drought and elevated carbon dioxide. These changes result in reduced growth and yield in many plants. However, it is clear that such responses vary in magnitude between species and also between different cultivars within species. The mechanisms by which some species and genotypes are protected from ozone injury are not clear, but may include differences in uptake into the leaf or in the various components of antioxidant metabolism. Ozone may also increase the severity of many fungal diseases, while virus infections reduce the effects of ozone in some plants.

Nitrous Oxides

The sensitivity of weed species' seeds to nitrous oxides has raised questions about the potential impact of air pollution on native plants. Nitrous oxides found in air pollution may trigger emergence of sensitive seeds during conditions that are unfavourable for their survival. Over time the seed bank might become depleted in these species, leading to a reduced likelihood of plant species regeneration. Over the long-term this can reduce total vegetation cover and increase erosion rates and other risks.

Past and Present Pollution

Acid depositions and ozone exposures have increased considerably in the past 50 years in Asia, Europe and the US, and there have been many reports of tree/forest decline and increased mortality. In general, the more highly polluted forests have the higher rate of decline and mortality.

Acidification by Forestry

While forestry has long been considered to be adversely affected by air pollution and acid rain, recent studies show it to be part of the acidifying process. The rough canopies of mature evergreen forests are efficient scavengers of particulate and gaseous contaminants in polluted air. This results in a more acidic deposition under the forest canopies than in open land. Chemical processes at the roots of trees, evergreens in particular, further acidify the soil and soil water in forest catchments. When the forests are located on poorly buffered soils, these processes can lead to a significant acidification of the run-off water and consequent damage to associated streams and lakes.

Conditions in urban environments place trees under numerous stresses including compacted soil, soil moisture extremes, and reduced soil fertility. Polluted air is another stress that contributes to the decline of urban trees. Air pollution may cause short-term (acute) damage, which is immediately visible, and long-term (chronic) damage, which can lead to gradual tree decline. Long-term damage may predispose trees to other disorders, making diagnosis difficult.

The major phytotoxic (toxic to plants) air pollutants, in decreasing order of severity, are:

- Oxidants [ozone and peroxyacetyl nitrate (PAN)]
- Sulfur dioxide
- Particulates

Gaseous Pollutants

Acute gaseous pollutant damage to red maple leaves. All leaves on the tree are chlorotic (pale yellow).

Gaseous pollutants, such as ozone and sulfur dioxide, enter plants through natural openings, usually stomates, and react within leaf tissues to inhibit photosynthesis. Acute damage levels can be high enough to cause sudden tissue damage and death. Chronic damage occurs when small amounts of toxic gases enter leaves and do not initially cause tissue death, but inhibit leaf functions. Whether or not a pollutant causes acute or chronic damage depends upon tree species. Individual trees within a species often display varying degrees of tolerance to the same pollutant.

Ozone

Ozone is the most damaging air pollutant. The action of sunlight (ultraviolet radiation) on molecular oxygen and oxides of nitrogen spontaneously generates ozone. The organic compounds in automobile exhaust enhance ozone accumulation. Ozone can move across great distances to cause tree damage far from its origin and is therefore classified as a non-point-source pollutant.

The extent of tree damage depends on the concentration of ozone, the duration of exposure, and tree sensitivity. Acute damage to deciduous trees causes marginal leaf burn and dot-like or irregularly shaped lesions or spots that may be tan, white, or dark brown, and that may spread over entire leaves. Another common symptom is bleaching of the upper leaf surface. Acute damage to conifers causes browning at the same point on all needles in a bundle (needle cluster).

Chronic damage occurs with repeated ozone absorption in amounts not high enough to cause sudden tissue death. Chronic symptoms include chlorosis (general yellowing), premature leaf drop, reduced growth, and progressive decline of tree health and vigor. Ozone damage also increases a tree's susceptibility to insect damage. As ozone restricts carbohydrate movement in leaves, the resulting higher sugar concentration makes the leaves more susceptible to insect attacks.

PAN is produced through the interaction of sunlight and power plant and/or automobile emissions. High levels of PAN and ozone are toxic to trees, but ozone is more abundant and injurious.

Sulfur dioxide

Sulfur dioxide is primarily a result of fossil fuel burning for electricity generation, and to a lesser degree, the processing of steel and other ores. Sulfur dioxide is classified as a point-source pollutant.

Acute sulfur dioxide damage causes severe leaf scorch, usually on upper interveinal leaf surfaces. Younger leaves are generally more sensitive. Moisture in the air or on leaf surfaces may combine with sulfur dioxide to form sulfuric acid. Sulfuric acid causes leaf scorch, spotting defoliation, and can also cause tree death over a large geographic area with many affected species. Chronic sulfur dioxide damage results in leaf chlorosis (colors of the chlorosis ranging from white to red) and tree decline.

Particulates

Particulates (dusts), classified as point-source pollutants, are generated by major industrial processes as well as by quarries, rock-crushing plants, cement plants, soil erosion, and auto exhaust emissions. Particulates are not extremely damaging, but can inhibit or reduce photosynthesis by plugging stomates. Particulates are usually washed from leaves by rain or irrigation, and are therefore more harmful during dry periods.

Weather and Pollutants

Air currents carry all air pollutants. Air movements and geographic features influence pollutant concentration, chemical structure, and the duration of tree exposure to pollutants.

Air temperature determines vertical movement of air pollutants. Under normal conditions, warm air near the soil surface causes pollutants to rise vertically. Pollutants rapidly become diluted and blown away by upper level winds before contacting many trees. However, thermal inversions (cool air at the surface beneath warmer air above) restrict movement and dispersal of pollutants, resulting in increasing phytotoxic levels and prolonged exposure. These inversions usually occur in narrow valleys close to mountain ranges, and near large bodies of water.

Temperature also influences a pollutant's chemical reaction rate. When the temperature is high, more photochemical oxidants are produced. These oxidants cause more severe damage during sunny hot weather and less damage during cool cloudy weather. Atmospheric moisture causes pollutants to become solutions, increasing their toxic potential.

Diagnosing Air Pollution Damage

Proper diagnosis of air pollution damage is difficult because other causes of tree damage, including environment, insects and diseases, can cause similar (mimicking) symptoms. Obtaining the following information will help in making a proper diagnosis:

1. Pollutant origin (point-of-source or non-point-of-source?)
2. Chemical and physical nature of the pollutant.
3. Geographic and topographic influences.
4. Weather conditions (air temperature and wind direction).

Trees with a range of ozone tolerance and sensitivity

Tolerant	Intermediate	Sensitive
Arborvitae (*Thuja* spp.)	Boxelder (*Acer negundo*)	Ash, white (*Fraxinus americana*)
Birch, European white (*Betula pendula*)	Elm, lacebark (*Ulmus parvifolia*)	Ash, green (*Fraxinus pennsylvanica*)
Dogwood, white (*Cornus florida*)	Gum, sweet (Liquidambar styraciflua)	Catalpa (*Catalpa* spp.)
Fir, balsam (*Abies balsamea*)	Lilac (*Syringa* spp.)	Crabapple (*Malus* spp.)
Fir, Douglas (*Pseudotsuga menziesii*)	Oak, black (*Quercus velutina*)	Honeylocust (*Gleditsia triacanthos*)
Fir, white (*Abies concolor*)	Oak, scarlet (*Quercus coccinea*)	Mountain ash, European (*Sorbus aucuparia*)
Ginkgo (*Ginkgo biloba*)	Pine, eastern white (*Pinus strobus*)	Oak, white (*Quercus alba*)
Gum, black (*Nyssa sylvatica*)	Pine, Scotch (*Pinus sylvestris*)	Oak, pin (*Quercus palustris*)
Holly (*Ilex* spp.)	Pine, shortleaf (*Pinus echinata*)	Pine, Austrian (*Pinus nigra*)
Linden, American (*Tilia americana*)	Redbud, eastern (*Cercis canadensis*)	Pine, Loblolly (*Pinus taeda*)
Linden, little-leaf (*Tilia cordata*)		Pine, Virginia (*Pinus virginiana*)
Maple, Norway (*Acer platanoides*)		Poplar, tulip (*Liriodendron tulipifera*)
Maple, sugar (*Acer saccharum*)		Sycamore, American (*Platanus occidentalis*)
Oak, English (*Quercus robur*)		Walnut, English (*Juglans regia*)
Oak, red (*Quercus rubra*)		Willow, weeping (*Salix babylonica*)
Pine, red (*Pinus resinosa*)		Zelkova, Japanese (*Zelkova serrata*)
Spruce, blue (*Picea pungens*)		
Spruce, Norway (*Picea abies*)		
Walnut, black (*Juglans nigra*)		
Yew (*Taxus* spp.)		

Trees with a range of sulfur dioxide tolerance and sensitivity

Tolerant	Intermediate	Sensitive
Arborvitae (*Thuja* spp.)	Linden, American (*Tilia americana*)	Ash, green (*Fraxinus pennsylvanica*)
Ginkgo (*Ginkgo biloba*)	Boxelder (*Acer negundo*)	Birch (*Betula* spp.)
Juniper (*Juniperus* spp.)	Cottonwood (*Populus deltoides*)	Elm, lacebark (*Ulmus parvifolia*)
Linden, littleleaf (*Tilia cordata*)	Elm, American (*Ulmus americana*)	Pine, eastern white (*Pinus strobus*)
Maple, silver (*Acer saccharinum*)	Lilac (*Syringa* spp.)	Poplar, lombardy (*Populus nigra* 'Italica')
Maple, sugar (*Acer saccharum*)	Maple, red (*Acer rubrum*)	Serviceberry (*Amelanchier* spp.)
Oak, pin (*Quercus palustris*)	Mountain ash, European (*Sorbus aucuparia*)	Willow, black (*Salix nigra*)
Oak, red (*Quercus rubra*)	Oak, white (*Quercus alba*)	
Spruce, blue (*Picea pungens*)	Pine, Austrian (*Pinus nigra*)	

5. Length of exposure and concentration.
6. Types of symptoms.
7. Possible mimicking symptoms.
8. Size of affected area.
9. Date of suspected exposure.
10. Affected tree and other species.
11. History of previous exposure.

Control of Air Pollution

Following methods are useful in controlling air pollution:

Occasionally Pollution control at source is not possible by preventing the emission of pollutants. Then it becomes necessary to install pollution control equipment to remove the gaseous pollutants from the main gas stream.

The pollution are present in high concentration at the source and as their distance form the source increase they become diluted by diffusion with environmental air.

Pollution equipments are generally classified into two types:

(a) Control devices for particulate contaminants

(b) Control devices for gaseous contaminants

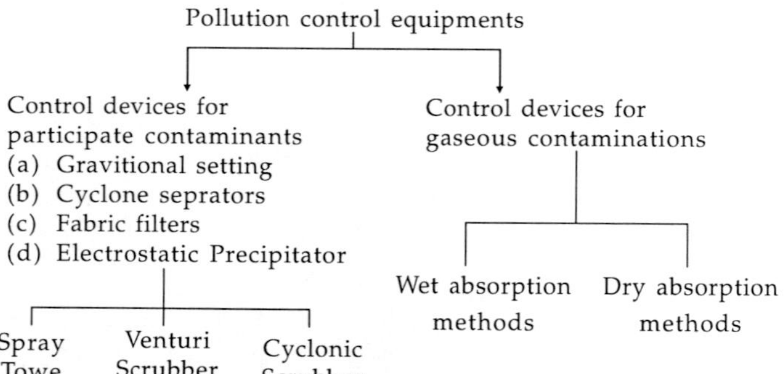

1. **Zoning:** A separate zone or area is set aside for industries thereby reducing the ill effects of air pollution on the urban dwellers.
2. **Control of air pollution at source:** The air pollution can be minimized at the source by the following four ways:
   (i) Changes by way of raw material
   (ii) Modification of process
   (iii) Alternations of particular equipments, components etc.
   (iv) Removal of pollutants at the sources
3. **Control of air pollution by devices:**

(A) For a gaseous pollutants

(a) Absorption

In this technique, the gases effluent are passed through scrubber or absorbers containing suitable liquid absorbent to remove of modify one or more of the pollutants present in it.

The efficiency of gas absorption process depend upon (a) the chemical reactivity of the gaseous pollutant in liquid phase (b) the extent of surface contact between the liquid and the gas (c) the contact time (d) the concentration of the absorbing medium.

The equipment used include plate tower, spray towers, packed tower, bubble-cap plate towers used to removing pollutants like NO_x, H_2S, SO_2, SO_3, and fluoride from gaseous pollutants.

Pollutants	Absorbent
NO_x	H_2O, Aq. HNO_3
HF	H_2O, NaOH
H_2S	Ethanol, NaOH + Phenol (3:2), Sodium alanine, Soda ash etc.
SO_2	Water, Alkaline water, Suspension of $Ca(OH)_2$, 1:1 mixture of water and xylidine

(b) Adsorption

In this technique, the gaseous effluents are passed through solid adsorbers taken in suitable containers. The organic or inorganic constituents of the effluent gaseous are held at the interface of the solid absorbent by physical adsorption or chemisorption.

The efficiency of adsorption depends upon the surface area per unit weight of the adsorbent, other physical and chemical characteristics of the adsorbent and nature and concentration of gas being used.

Following are the common adsorbent used are:

Pollutants	Adsorption
NOx	Silica gel, commercial Zeolite
HF	Lump lime stone, Porous pellets of NaF, Iron oxides
SO_2	Pulverized lime stone or dolomite, alkaline or dolomite, alkalized aluminum (Al_2O_3 + $NaNO_2$)
Organic solvent vapor	Activated carbon
Petroleum Fractions	Bauxite
Vapor associated with gases	Aluminum, silica gel, Bauxite

(c) Combustion

The burning of any substance, in gaseous, liquid, or solid form. In its broad definition, combustion includes fast exothermic chemical reactions, generally in the gas phase but not excluding the reaction of solid carbon with a gaseous oxidant. Flames represent combustion reactions that can propagate through space at subsonic velocity and are accompanied by the emission of light. The flame is the result of complex interactions of chemical and physical processes whose quantitative description must draw on a wide range of disciplines, such as chemistry, thermodynamics, fluid dynamics, and molecular physics. In the course of the chemical reaction, energy is released in the form of heat, and atoms and free radicals, all highly reactive intermediates of the combustion reactions, are generated.

Combustion process like flame combustion or catalytic combustion can be utilized to greatest advantages when the gases or vapors to be controlled are organic in nature. Equipment employing the principle of flame combustion includes:

(i) Fume and vapor incineration

(ii) After-burners

(iii) Flare, either with steam injection or venture flare

(d) Modification of the Process

In some cases a change in the process, either by way in the composition of process materials or removal of impurities may help in odour control. Methods include substitution of low-odour solvents for highly odorous ones, adjustment of process variables like temperature, residence time etc.

(B) For particulate emission

(i) Mechanical devices:

It mostly operates on the basis of flowing two mechanism:

(a) Gravity settling: In which the velocity of horizontal carrier gas is reduced adequately so that particles settle by gravitational force.

(b) Sudden change in the direction: sudden change in the direction of the gas flow causes the particles to separate out due to their grater momentum.

(c) Cyclone separator: Instead of gravitational force, centrifugal force is utilized by cyclone separators, to seprate the particulate matter from the pollutant gase.

Typically used to remove particulate from a gas stream, the gas enters tangentially at the top of a cylinder and is forced downward into a spiral motion. The particles exit the bottom while the gas turns upward into the vortex and leaves through the top of the unit. Pressure drops through cyclones are usually from 13 to 17 mm water gauge. Although seldom adequate by themselves, cyclone separators are often an effective first step in pollution control.

(d) Electrostatic precipitator

The electrostatic precipitator work on the principle of electrostatic precipitation i.e., electric charged particles present in the polluted gas are separated form the gas stream under the influence of electric field.

Major pollution control activities in India:

- Policy initiatives to improve environment like the National Conservation Strategy and Policy Statement for Environment & Development, 1992, Policy Statement for Abatement of Pollution, 1992
- National Forest Policy, 1988
- Notification and implementation of emission and effluent standards for air, water and noise levels
- Standards are formulated by a multidisciplinary group keeping in view the international standards, existing technologies and impact on health and environment
- Identification and Action Plans for 17 categories of major polluting industries
- Identification of 24 critically polluted areas for pollution abatement and improving environment
- Use of beneficiated coal with an ash content not exceeding 34% irrespective of their distance from pit head
- Action Plans for 141 polluted river stretches to improve quality of river water
- For controlling vehicular pollution, progressive emission norms at the manufacturing stage have been notified, cleaner fuels like unleaded petrol, low sulphur diesel and compressed natural gas (CNG) introduced
- Identification of clean technologies for large industries and clean technologies/processes for small scale industries
- Setting up of 'Common Effluent Treatment Plants (CETPs) for clusters of SSI units
- Implementation of an Eco-mark scheme to encourage production/consumption of environment–friendly products.

- Preparation of a Zoning Atlas, indicating status of the environment at district levels to guide environmentally sound location/siting of industries.
- Mandatory submission of annual Environmental Statement which could be extended into environmental audit.
- Initiation of environmental epidemiological studies in seven critically polluted areas to study the impact of environment on health.
- Setting up of authorities like the Environment Pollution (Prevention & Control) Authority for the National Capital Region for protecting and improving the quality of environment and preventing, controlling and abating environmental pollution.
- Provision of fiscal incentives for installation of Pollution control equipment and also for shifting of industries from congested areas.

With regard to pollution control, Indian Government enforces the following legislations to save the environmental pollution:

- Water (Prevention & Control of Pollution) Act, 1974 as amended in 1978 and 1988;
- Water (Prevention & Control of Pollution) Cess Act, 1977 as amended in 1991;
- Air (Prevention & Control of Pollution) Act, 1981 as amended in1987;
- Environment (Protection) Act, 1986;
- Hazardous Wastes (Management and Handling) Rules, 1989;
- Manufacture, Storage and Import of Hazardous Chemical Rules, 1989;
- The Environmental Impact Assessment Notification, 1994; and
- Bio-Medical Waste (Management & Handling) Rules, 1998.

Air Pollution from Automobiles

The automotive industry has made steady improvements in the area of fuel efficiency, and they promise more improvements to come. Automotive engineers have cut the weight of cars in half in the last 25 years. The miles-per-gallon rating of passenger cars has improved 39 percent in the last ten years. Unfortunately, fuel consumption has increased by 19 percent. According to Vital Signs, the increased emissions from the world's vehicles lead to global warming, acid rain, smog, and the disastrous health effects of air pollution. The internal combustion engines in cars produce oxides that combine with water vapor in the air to form acid rain. Smog is formed from the chemical reaction between unburned hydrocarbons and the oxides of nitrogen in automobile exhaust. The ton of carbon dioxide produced by burning gasoline is the leading cause of the greenhouse effect, which causes global warming. Vehicles contribute to an estimated 60-70 percent of urban air pollution. Automobiles do not maximize the energy they are producing, creating unnecessary waste. The largest area of needed improvement in the automobile is energy efficiency. Only 13 percent of the energy used by today's vehicles is used for propulsion. The most promising solution to this problem is alternative fuel vehicles.

Table 5.1 showing the effects and sources of pollutants will drive home the seriousness and urgency of the matter.

Table 5.1

Pollutants	Sources	Effects
Carbon Monoxide (CO)	Automobiles, trucks, heavy vehicles, construction and industrial equipment.	Affects the oxygenation of tissues. It causes headaches, and decreased mental alertness.
Lead (Pb)	Leaded Petrol	Brain damage and kidney damage. Children exposed to this pollutant often acquire learning disabilities.
Nitrogen Oxides (NOx)	Automobiles	Respiratory infections and lung damage. Retards the growth of plants. Reacts with certain atmospheric elements to form acid rain.
Ozone (O_3)	Formed when NOx and organic compounds react in the presence of sunlight.	Irritates the nose and throat, and causes headaches. It also damages vegetation.
Particulate Matter	Caused by the incomplete combustion of any fuel.	Causes respiratory disorders and lung damage. It is also a suspected carcinogen.
Sulphur Dioxide (SO_2)	Produced when fossil fuels are burnt.	Causes lung diseases and breathing problems for asthmatics. It also forms acid rain.
Volatile Organic Compounds	Produced by automobiles and the use of solvents.	Respiratory disorders and carcinogenic effects caused by benzene.

Automobile comprises Particulate Matter, Respirable Dust Particles, Nitrogen Oxide, Sulphur Dioxide, Carbon Monoxide and Lead. A health examination of the city's traffic policemen done recently has revealed that vehicular pollution has done irreparable damage to their lungs and leads to respiratory disorders. Further tests with pulmonary function test apparatus are on the cards.

This straight away throws to focus the urgent need to promote alternate fuel systems that lower the pollution levels and are also cost effective to run. For those who blame it all on diesel vehicles alone, here is some news about petrol. The benzene emissions from petrol vehicles are as carcinogenic as suspended particulate matter and nitrogen oxides in diesel. Therefore, the natural choice falls on Liquefied Petroleum Gas (LPG) that is termed as Autogas when used to propel vehicles. Though there is a perceptible shift in politics over this issue with over 40 cities in India seeking a ban on non-clean vehicles, still much has to be done, as manufacturers even now await Government clearance through Gazette Notification to commercially produce vehicles with alternative fuel sources like LPG.

In the case of LPG, there is hardly any discharge of carbon monoxide and exhaust fumes contain less harmful substances compared to petrol and diesel. Thus the environmental advantages of Autogas are indisputable.

Control of Air Pollution from Automobiles

The development of effective motor vehicle controls require a thorough understanding of emission production process in the gasoline – powered, spark-ignition, internal combustion engine (ICE). In operation gasoline is pumped from a fuel tank to a carburetor where it is mixed with air. The cycle begins as the air – fuel mixture is drawn or injected into a combustion chamber (cylinder). The subsequent upward movement of the piston compresses the air-fuel mixture to the design compression ratio, where it is spark lignite. On ignition, the explosion of the gasoline forces the piston downward, providing power to the drive shaft which propels the vehicle. The hot combustion gases are vented through the exhaust port into the exhaust port into the exhaust manifold during the upward movement of the piston. The cycle is continuously repeated in each cylinder.

Motor vehicles emissions are generated in several different ways and locations during engine/vehicle operation. The most important sources are, of course, those produced in combustion and vented through the exhaust pipe. These exhaust gases consist mainly of unburned HCs, CO, and NOx and account for approximately 90-92% of all motor vehicle emission. Some products of combustion are not vented through the exhaust system, as they slip by the piston rings and the cylinder walls. These "blowby" gases mainly of unburned HCs that accumulate in the crankcase. In uncontrolled vehicles they would normally be vented to the atmosphere through a crankcase exhaust port. A third source of emission is the volatilization of HCs through the carburetor and fuel tank vents. Carburetor emission are pronounced during the "hot soak" period immediately following vehicle operation.

Combustion Chemistry

Gasoline basically consists of a mixture of no-methane HC compounds that, when ignited in the presence of sufficient O_2, producers H_2O, CO_2, and energy.

$$C_8H_{18} + 12.5\ O_2 + 47\ N_2 \rightarrow 8\ CO_2 + 47\ N_2 + 9\ H_2O$$

On the basis of these reactions, 1735 g of air are required for every 114 g of gasoline for complete combustion. In theory, complete combustion will occur at an air-fuel (A/F) ratio of 15:1:1, or the stoichiometric ratio. The actual ratio in an operative vehicle may vary considerably. Prior to emission control requirements, ration of 12.5 to 14:1 were common. The rich A/F ratios provide maximum power output. Because of insufficient O_2, rich A/F mixtures generates large quantities of CO and HCs. Note the minimum CO emission are produced near the stoichiometric ratio.

Carbon monoxide is produced by incomplete combustion, the degree of which is determined by the A/F ratio. Although A/F ratio also affects emissions of unburned HCs, the primary source of HC emission is the quenching of the combustion reaction as the flame front of burning fuel approaches the relatively cool walls of the cylinder. This quenching permits a film of unburned or partially burned gasoline a few thousandths of an inch (25 to 50 μm) wide to remain near the cylinder walls during the combustion phase of engine operation. This unburned fuel is expelled in the exhaust with other combustion gases. Because of the high combustion chamber temperature (> 1350° C) O_2 and N_2 may combine to form NOx.

Crankcase Blow by Gases

Crankcase emission can be controlled by a relatively simple and inexpensive technology called positive crankcase ventilation. In this control technique, blow by gases are circulated to the combustion chamber for re-burning.

Evaporation Emission

Evaporative emission includes diurnal, hot soak, and running losses. Diurnal emission occurs as the fuel tank of a parked vehicle takes in air as it cools at night and exhales air and gasoline vapors as it heats up during the day. Hot soak emissions occur after the engine is shut off as heat from the engine heats the fuel system. Running losses occur when gasoline vapors are forced from the fuel tank while the vehicle is being operated and the fuel tank becomes hot. Evaporative losses can also occur during refueling.

Evaporation emission control charcoal canisters sorb gasoline vapors. Sorbed vapors are purged from charcoal into the engine during normal driving.

Exhaust Gases

Unlike blowby gases and evaporative emission, which are controlled by relative simple and inexpensive technologies, exhaust gas emission have proven to be more difficult to control. The complexity of the exhaust gas problem is increased by the fact that control measures employed to reduce emissions may significantly affect vehicle operating characteristics to which consumers are particularly sensitive. These include vehicle power, driveability, and fuel economy. Adding further to the dilemma is the paradox of CO/HC and NOx control measures. In general, measures employed to control CO/HC increase NOx; conversely NOx control measures may increase CO and HC.

Dispersion of Air Pollutants

The constantly moving atmosphere provides and enormous sink of the dispersal of air pollutants. However, when pollutants are first released from a source, their concentrations are usually high, and effects on environmental quality may be immediate. Dispersion must take place quickly in a limited portion of the atmosphere. Initially, dispersion is influenced by micro- and mesoscale motion. Macroscale motions disperse substances with long atmospheric residue time, such as carbon dioxide (CO_2) and chlorofulurocarbons (CFCs), throught the troposphere. Scales of air motion and characteristic phenomenon associated with them are summarized in table:

Scale	Geographical area (mi)	Time period	Meteorological phenomenon
Macroscale	> 100	Weeks-motions	Atmospheric circulation, weather fronts, high and low pressure system, Hurricanes
Mesoscale	10-100	Hrs-days	Land/sea breeze, valley winds, urban heat islands
Microscale	< 10	Min	Plume behaviour, Builidng downwash and eddy curents

Micro - and Macroscale Dispersion of Pollutants

In the initial dispersion process form point or area sources, pollutants are released into the ambient environment where their transport and subsequent dilution depend on local meteorological phenomena and the influence of topography. In these local dispersion processes important meteorological phenomena include wind (speed and direction), turbulence and atmospheric stability.

Wind

Horizontal winds play a singnificant role in the transport and dilution of pollutnts. As the wind speed increases, the volme of air moving by a source in a given period of time also increase. If the emission rate is relatively constant, a doubling of the wind speed will have the pollutant concentration, as the concentration is an inverse function of the wind speed.

The speed of the horizontal wind is affected by friction, which is proportional to surface roughness, which is determined by topographical features such as mountains, valley, rivers, lakes, forests, cultivated fields, and buildings. Wind speed over smooth surface, e.g., cultivated fields and lakes, tend to be on the average higher than those over rougher surface, e.g. mountain and buildings. Surface roughness associated with urban areas increases, wind speeds near the surface are significantly reduced.

Pollutant dispersion is also significantly affected by variability in wind direction. If wind direction is relatively constant the same area will be continuously exposed to high pollutant levels. If, one the other hand, wind direction is constantly shifting, pollutants will be dispersed over a large area and concentrations over any given exposed area are lower. Large changes in wind direction may occur over short periods of time.

Turbulence

Air does not flow smoothly near the earth's surface, it follows patterns of three-dimensional movement called turbulence. Turbulent eddies are produced by tow specific process: (1) thermal turbulence, resulting form atmospheric heating and (2) mechanical turbulence caused by the movement of air past an obstruction. Usually both types of turbulence occur in any given atmospheric situation, although in some situations one or the other may prevail. Thermal turbulence is dominated on clear, sunny days with light winds. Although mechanical turbulence occurs under a variety of atmospheric conditions, it is dominant on windy nights with neutral atmospheric stability. The effect of turbulence is to enhance the dispersion process, although in the case of mechanical turbulence, downwards from the pollution source may result in high pollution levels immediately downwind.

Lapse Rate and Atmospheric Stability

In the atmosphere, the temperature decreases with height up to an elevation of approximately 10 km. This decrease is due to the reduction of heating process with height and radiative cooling of air, and reaches it maximum in the upper levels of the troposphere. The temperature decrease with height is described by the lapse rate. On the average, temperature decreases - 0.65° C/100 m or – 6.5°C/km. This is the normal lapse rate.

If a parcel of dry air were lifted in a dry environment, it would undergo adiabatic lapse expansion and cool. This adiabatic cooling would result in a lapse rate of – 1° C/100 m or – 10° C/100 km, the dry adiabatic lapse rate.

Individual temperature measurement in the vertical may vary considerably from either the normal or dry adiabatic lapse rate. This change of temperature with height for any given measurement is the environmental lapse rate. Values for environmental laps rates characterize the stability of the atmosphere and profoundly affect vertical air motion and the dispersion of pollutants.

The relationship of environmental lapse rate to stability is illustrated. When there are no source or sink of thermal energy the temperature of a rising air parcel will decrease with heights at a rate of – 1° C/100 m, or the dry adiabatic lapse rate. If a parcel of warm air released into an environment where the temperature decrease with heights is greater than the adiabatic lapse rate, say -2° C/100 m, the parcel will rise rapidly. The atmosphere will be unstable and conditions for the vertical dispersion of pollutants will be excellent. This is a super adiabatic lapse rate.

If a warm parcel of air is placed in an environmental where the lapse rate approaches the adiabatic lapse rate (fig), the decrease of temperature with height would be the same as the cooling rate of the parcel and the atmosphere would be neutrally stable. The parcel then would always be warmer than its surroundings and, as a results, it would rise completely through the neutral layer. Good dispersion of air pollutants is achieved in a neutrally stable environment.

If a warm parcel of air were released into an environment in which the temperature remained constant with heights, i.e. were isothermal (fig), it would rise until it reached equilibrium with the temperature of its surroundings. Under isothermal conditions the atmosphere tends to be more sable and the dispersion of pollutants becomes somewhat limited or moderate.

If warm parcel of air is released into an environment where the temperature in inverted (fig), that is, as temperature increase with height, it will rise until the temperature and density are in equilibrium with the environment. if the parcel temperature is cooler than its surroundings, the parcel will sink. In an inversion, atmospheric conditions are very stable, that is, they tend to resist change, and vertical motions are restricted. Dispersion potential under inversion conditions is very poor.

Using the neutral or dry adiabatic lapse rate with its good dispersion characteristics as a reference point, we can characterize the dispersion characteristics of other environmental lapse rate; dispersion characteristics are good to excellent. The greater the deviation to the left, the more unstable the atmosphere and the more enhanced dispersion. Moving to the right of the dry adiabatic lapse rate, the atmosphere become stable and dispersion become more limited. The grater the deviation to the right from the adiabatic lapse rate, the more stable the atmosphere and the poorer the dispersion potential.

Mixing Height

Movement of air in the vertical dimensions is enhanced by vertical temperature differences. The steeper the temperature gradient, the more vigorous the convective and turbulent mixing of the atmosphere. The larger the vertical column in which turbulent mixing occurs, the more effective the dispersion process.

The maximum mixing heights (MMH), or maximum mixing depth (MMD), is the depth of the convective layer associated with the maximum surface temperature.

The MMH shows diurnal and seasonal variations. In addition, it is markedly affected by topography and macroscale air circulation (anticyclones). During the day, minimum MMH values occur just before sunrise. As solar energy heats up the ground and warms the air, it extends, becomes less dense, and rises by convection. Cooler air from aloft descends to take it place (fig). As solar heating continues, vertical motions become intense and the MMH is reached in early afternoon, with values of several thousand meters. The minimum vales of MMH, observes at nights and in the early morning hours, may be a result of surface level inversions produced by the radiative cooling of the ground and the air on clear nights. In these situations the MMH may be near zero. These surface level inversions are particularly intense in mountain valleys. The MMH shows seasonal variability with maximum values in the summer and minimum vales in late fall and winter. Fortunately, however, the lower MMHs of winter are associated with higher average surface winds speeds. As a result dispersion is not as adversely affected.

Topographical features such as water surface with their large heat absorbing capacities results in lower MMHs. Land surfaces with little vegetative cover e.g. desert: may have mixing heights of 5000 m or more. MMH is affected by macroscale air motions as well. Subsidence inversions produced in semipermanent marine high pressure systems and stagnating migratory anticyclones significantly reduce the MMH.

Air Pollution Analysis

Introduction

The measurement of the concentrations of air pollutants is essential for formulating the air quality standards and to know the surrounding air quality status. Great progress has been made in recent years in developing techniques of monitoring air pollutants. Monitoring is an essential component in the effort to control and understand the effects of pollution, even though the measurement of levels of pollution does nothing in itself to make to air any safer. However levels of pollutants in the atmosphere is governed by various factors such as atmospheric conditions which have profound effects on pollution and its harmfulness, and meteorology play an important the transport of pollutants from sources to receptors. Pollutants emitted into the atmosphere are subject to four types of effects: transport, dilution, modification, and removal. A full analysis of the "Fate of pollutants" entering the atmosphere would incorporate all four of these effects. Moreover the first two effects, (i.e.) the transport and dilution cause the dispersion of pollutants in the atmosphere. Therefore consideration of meteorological factors is also an important in ambient air quality monitoring.

The basic source of difficulty with measuring ambient levels of pollutants is the fact that they ordinarily occur at very low concentrations. Most gaseous pollutants occur at levels below 1 ppm by volume, corresponding roughly to a mass concentration of less than one milligram per cubic metre of air and the particulate matter is generally found with a mass concentration of much less than 100 milligram per cubic metre of air.

Accurate measurement of pollutant concentration at ambient levels requires sophisticated techniques and instrumentation. Only recently such techniques and instruments have been development which offer much promise. Analytical instruments can be classified into two classes. The first class of instruments includes the measurement of some physical property directly of the pollutants. Infrared spectrometer is an example.

Here the amount of infrared radiation absorbed by specific pollutants is detected. The second class is the chemicophysical type instruments where the pollutant being measured first undergoes chemical transformation and the product of the reaction is then measured by using an appropriate analytical technique. As an example, the classic "wet" chemical techniques are all chemicophysical. In these a sample of pollutant is collected for a period of time in a liquid absorber. The sample is then reacted with another agent, resulting in a change in color or in the formation of another product. The intensity of the color or the concentration of the products is related to the concentration of the original pollutant.

Measurements are generally made on a continuous, discrete, or average time basis. The first and most desirable type of measurement is continuous and is carried out with instruments having very fast response times, such as infrared spectrometers. In discrete type of measurement, the sample is injected into the instrument of discrete procedure. Monitoring devices which require a pollutant to be collected over a finite period of time in order to obtain measurable concentrations yield integrated or averaged results. Most wet techniques operate on this principle. Such methods are insensitive to short-term variations in concentration.

Ambient Air Quality Monitoring

Measurements of air pollution are classified dependent upon the following criteria:

(i) The exhaustion quantity (or concentration) of each pollutant from emission sources

(ii) Effectiveness test of pollution prevention equipments: Capture of the actual conditions and trend

(iii) Environmental pollution

(iv) Effects of air pollution on the human body, living things and others

(v) Relationship between air pollution and atmospheric phenomena

(vi) Forecast of air pollution

Monitoring of Ambient Air

Conditions for the Set-up of Monitoring Station

The purpose of monitoring stations is to collect the necessary basic information for implementation of proper measures to keep the local environmental air always clean. Hence, each monitoring station must be provided with the following four functions:

(i) To offer adequate data to determine whether or not the related air quality standards are being accomplished.

(ii) Capability for rapid collection and delivery of the necessary information so that smooth emergency action can be taken to prevent air pollution episode.

(iii) Capability of comprehending the general trend of air pollution over the entire area; background concentration data is essential for this purpose.

(iv) To offer useful data to evaluate land utilization plans in urban areas, public transportation construction plans, and new air pollution control measures.

Measurement Items at Monitoring Station

The measurement items at the monitoring station varies according to the purposes. The general atmospheric environment monitoring items are SO_2, NOx, CO, oxidant and suspended particulate matter (SPM). Particularly for the purpose to investigate pollution caused by industries main items are SO_2, NOx, (i.e., NO+NO_2) and SPM. The environmental assessment for the location of a factory is commonly carried out regarding these 3 items. Other particular pollutants (such as hydrocarbons, HF, HCI, CO, etc.) will be added as occasional demands. The major artificial sources of each pollutant are presented in table 8.1.

Table 8.1: Major artificial sources of pollutants

Substance	Emission source facilities, etc.
Sox	Various types of boilers, chemicals plants, diesel cars, vessels, coal heating, etc.
NOx	Various types of combustion facilities, chemical plants, furnaces, automobiles, vessels, aircrafts, home heating, etc.
Suspended particulate (SPM) Total suspended particulate (TSPM)	Various types of boilers, furnaces, various manufacturing devices accompanying dust generation, automobiles, vessels, air-crafts, civil engineering, stock yard of coal
Hydrocarbons (HC)	Petrochemical plant, oil-storage tank, painting and coating, automobiles, vessels, air crafts, etc.
HCl, Cl_2	Garbage incinerators, HCl manufacturing
HF	Manufacturing facilities of aluminum, glass, phosphate fertilizer, phosphoric acid, fluoric resins, etc.
CO	Automobiles
Offensive odor	Live-stock raising, food processing, paper and pulp mill, fertilizers, refuse disposal, leather manufacturing, chemical industry

It is also necessary to measure wind direction, wind speed, temperature, humidity, solar radiation, and other meteorological observations, along with AAQ Monitoring for interpretation of AAQ results. The Ambient Air Quality standard given by CPCB are as follows.

Pollutants	Industrial Area (μg/m³)	Residential and Commercial (μg/m³)	Sensitive Area (μg/m³)
SPM	500	200	100
RPM	150	75	-
SO_2	120	80	30
NOx	120	80	30
CO	5000	2000	1000

In Japan, environment standards of ambient air have been established for such 5 items as SO_2, NOx, CO, photochemical oxidant and suspended particulate matters (SPM), with their respective designated measurement methods being stipulated.

Background Connection

Air pollution should be discussed by comparing the concentrations of air pollutants with those of gaseous and particulate matter contained in the air over a "clean" area where the artificial activities are not observed. Hence, background concentrations must be measured in advance as a reference for comparison.

Location of Monitoring Stations

Each monitoring station must be able to grasp the level of air pollution and the pattern of its changes over the entire area it covers. Its covering range must be determined in the light of meteorological conditions, topographical features, and the distribution of pollution sources in that area.

Take a gaseous pollutant, such as SO_2 for example, which is emitted by combustion process. In areas crowded with pollution sources, such as industrial zones and the downtown areas of large cities where many high-storied buildings are located, the representative pattern of air pollution may be grasped by covering an area about 3 km in radius. On the other hand a broader area about 5 to 10 km in radius can be covered for residential and other less polluted area.

Number of Monitoring Stations

When selecting the location of a monitoring station, the following factors must be considered:

- In a densely polluted area, a station must be located for each zone in the area that represents the characteristic air pollution pattern (usually an area of 6 km in diameter).
- Additional stations must be set on the periphery of that zone to monitor the amount of pollutions entering that zone from outside.
- Monitoring stations must be arranged taking future land utilization plans into consideration.
- Monitoring stations must be arranged in a proper manner to effectively evaluate the air pollution control measures being planned.

Except these fixed stations to monitor ambient air as a whole, it is necessary to have a mobile station which is a vehicle carrying a measuring kit and a monitoring station specially installed for automobile exhaust gas measurement. The latter is usually located at the side of motorway and its items of measurement are limited to CO_2, NOx and hydrocarbons. A temporary station is also set in some situations.

The integrated air pollution monitoring station must be equipped with following analyzers and instruments SO_2, NOx, CO, hydrocarbon and oxidant analyzers, high and low-volume air samplers, and meteorological instruments to monitor wind velocity, wind direction, atmospheric temperature, solar radiation intensity, etc. The following factors must be taken into consideration when selecting the AAQ location.

(i) There must be no stacks, vent pipes or any other facilities that emit pollutants around the premises.

(ii) In order to prevent the effects from a turbulent flow in any direction, the air sampling port must be at least 3 meters away from a building and other obstructions.

Air must be collected at a position about 6 meters above the ground (more than 1.5 meters and, in any case, less than 10 meters) to prevent the effects from buildings and trees as well as to prevent the entry of dust and dirt from the ground. When measuring air pollutants of automotive exhaust gases, sample air must be collected at a place about 3 meters above the ground level.

Method used in AAQ Monitoring

Parameter	Technique	Technical Protocol	Minimum Detectable Limit ($\mu g/m^3$)
Suspended Particulate Matter	High volume sampler/ Respirable Dust Sampler (Gravimetric method)	IS-5182 (Part-IV)	5.0
Respirable Particulate Matter	Respirable Dust Sampler (Gravimetric method)	IS-5182 (Part-IV)	5.0
Sulphur Dioxide	West and Gaeke	IS-5182 (Part-II)	0.5
Oxides of Nitrogen	Jacob & Hochheiser	IS-5182 (Part-IV)	0.5

Measurement of Air Pollutants

(a) Oxides of Nitrogen oxide as NO_2 (*Modified Jacobs - Hochheiser method*)

Principle: Nitrogen oxides as Nitrogen dioxide are collected by bubbling air through sodium hydroxide solution to form a stable solution of sodium nitrite. The nitrite ion produced during sampling is determined colorimetrically by reacting the exposed absorbing reagent with phosphoric acid, sulphanilamide, and N (1-napthyl) ethylendiamine dihydrochloride. The method is applicable to collection of 24 hours samples in the field and subsequent analysis in the laboratory.

Range and Sensitivity

The range of the analysis is 0.01 to 1.5 µg NO_2/ml. with 50 ml absorbing reagent and a sampling rate of 200 ml/min for 24 hour, the range of the method is 20 to 740 μg/m^3 (0.01 to 0.4 ppm) nitrogen dioxide. A concentration of 0.01 μg oxides of nitrogen (as NO_2/ml.) will produce an absorbance of 0.005 using 1-cm cells.

Reagents

1. **Absorbing reagent:** Dissolve 4.0 g of sodium hydroxide in distilled water and dilute to 1000 ml.
2. **Sulphanilamide:** Dissolve 20 gm of sulphanilamide in 700 ml of distilled water. Add with mixing, 50 ml of concentrated phosphoric acid (58 percent) and dilute to 1000 ml. This solution is stable for a month if refrigerated and protected from light.
3. **Hydrogen peroxide:** Dilute 0.2 ml of 30 percent hydrogen peroxide to 250 ml with distilled water. This solution may be used for a month if protected from light.
4. **Standard Nitrite Solution:** Dissolve sufficient desiccated sodium nitrite [$NaNO_2$ (assay of 97 percent or greater)] and dilute with distilled water to 1000 ml so that a solution containing 1000 μg NO_2 per ml is obtained. The amount of sodium nitrite is calculated as follows:

$$G = \frac{1.5}{A} \times 1000$$

Where:

G = amount in g of sodium nitrite,

1.5 = gravimetric factor converting NO_2 into nitrites and

A = assay, percent.

Procedure

Sampling

Assemble the sampling train including the absorber, critical flow control device and pump. Add 50 ml absorbing reagent to the absorber. Disconnect funnel, insert calibrated flow meter, and measure flow before sampling.

Analysis

Replace water lost by evaporation during sampling. Pipette 10 ml of the collected sample into a test tube, add 1.0

ml of hydrogen peroxide solution, 10.0 ml of sulphanilamide solution, and 1.4 NEDA solutions with mixing after the addition of each reagent. Prepare a blank in the same manner using 10 ml of absorbing reagent. After 10 minutes of color development interval, measure the absorbance at 540 nm against the blank. Read µg NO_2/ml from the standard curve.

Calibration Curve

Dilute 5.0 ml of the 1000 µg NO_2/ml solution to 200 ml with absorbing reagent. This solution contains 25 µg NO_2/ml. Pipette 1, 2, 5 and 15 ml of the 25 µg NO_2/ml solution into 50, 50, 100 and 250 volumetric flasks and dilute to the mark with absorbing reagent. The solutions contain 0.50, 1.00, 1.25, and 1.50 µg NO_2/ml, respectively. Run standards as instructed in analysis method. Plot the graph absorbance versus µg NO_2/ml.

Calculation

Calculate the volume of air sampled as follows:

$$V = \frac{F_1 + F_2}{2} \times T \times 10^{-6}$$

Where:

V = volume of air sampled, m^2,

F_1 = measured flow rate before sampling, ml/min,

F_2 = measured flow rate after sampling, ml/min and

T = time of sampling, min.

Calculate the concentration of nitrogen dioxide as follows:

$$\text{Mass of nitrogen dioxide in } \mu g/m^3 = \frac{(\mu g\ NO_2/ml) \times 50}{V \times 0.35}$$

Where:

50 = volume of absorbing reagent used in sampling ml,

V = volume of air sampled, m^3 and

0.35 = overall average efficiency.

(b) Sulphur dioxide SO_2, (*Modified West and Gaeke method*)

Principle: Sulphur dioxide in air is absorbed in a solution of potassium tetrachloro-mercurate (TCM). A dichlorosulphitomercurate complex, which resists oxidation by the oxygen in the air, is formed. Once formed, this complex is stable to strong oxidations such as ozone and oxides of nitrogen and therefore, the absorber solution may be stored for some time prior to analysis. The complex is made to react with pararosaniline and formaldehyde to form the intensity colored pararosaniline methylsulphonic acid. The absorbance of the solution is measured by means of a suitable spectrophotometer.

Interferences: The effects of the principal known interferences have been minimized or eliminated. Interferences by oxides of nitrogen are eliminated by sulphamic acid. Ozone is made to decompose by allowing the solution to stand for some time prior to analysis. The interferences of trace metals may be eliminated by the addition of ethlenediamine tetra acetic acid (EDTA) to the absorbing solution prior to sampling. At least 60 µg iron (III), 10 µg manganese (II), and 10 µg chromium (III) in 10 ml absorbing reagent can be tolerated in the procedure. No significant interference was found from 10 µg copper (II) and 22 µg vanadium (V). Ammonium, sulphide, and aldehydes do not interfere.

Reagents

1. **Absorbing reagent, 0.04 M Potassium Tetrachloro mercurate (TCM):** Dissolve 10.86 g mercuric chloride, 0.066 EDTA, and 6.0 g potassium chloride or sodium chloride 4.68 gm in water and bring to the mark in a 1 litre volumetric flask. The absorbing reagent is normally stable for six months. If a precipitate forms, discard the reagent after recovering the mercury.
2. **Sulphamic Acid (0.6 %):** Dissolve 0.6 g sulphamic acid in 100 ml distilled water, prepare fresh daily.

3. **Formaldeyde (0.2%):** Dilute 5 ml formaldehyde solution (36-38%) to 1 litre with distilled water, prepare freshly.
4. **Stock iodine solution (0.1 N):** Place 12.7 g iodine in a 250 ml beaker, add 40 g potassium iodide and 25 ml water. Stir until all is dissolved, then dilute to 1 litre with distilled water.
5. **Iodine solution (0.01 N):** Prepare approximately 0.01 N iodine solution by diluting 50 ml of stock solution to 500 ml with distilled water.
6. **Starch indicator solution:** Titrate 0.4 gm soluble starch and 0.002 g mercuric iodide preservative with a little water and add the paste slowly to 200 ml boiling water. Continue boiling until the solution is clear, cool, and transfer to a glass-coppered bottle.
7. **Stock sodium Thiosulfate solution (0.1 N):** Prepare a stock solution by placing 25 g sodium thiosulphate pentahydrate in a beaker, add 0.1 g sodium carbonate and dissolve using boiled, cooled distilled water making the solution up to a final volume of 1 litre. Allow the solution to stand one day before standardizing.

   To standardize, accurately weigh to the nearest 0.1 mg, 1.5 g primary standard potassium iodate dried at 180° C, dissolve, and dilute to the volume in a 500 ml volumetric flask. Into a 500 ml iodine flask, transfer 50 ml of iodate solution by pipette. Add 2 g potassium iodide and 10 ml of N hydrochloric acid and stopper the flask. After 5 min, titrate with stock thiosulfate solution to a pale yellow. Add 5 ml starch indicator solution and continue the titration until the blue color disappears. Calculate the normality of the stock solution.
8. **Sodium Thiosulphate (0.01 N):** Dilute 100 ml of the stock thiosulfate solution to 1 litre with freshly boiled and cooled distilled water.
9. **Standardized sulphite solution for preparation of working sulphite - TCM Solution:** Dissolve 0.30 g sodium metabisulphite ($Na_2S_2O_5$) or 0.40 g sodium

sulphite (Na_2SO_3) in 500 ml of recently boiled, cooled, distilled water. Sulphite solution is unstable, it is therefore important to use water of the highest purity to minimize this instability. This solution contains the equivalent of 320-400 μg/ml of SO_2. The actual concentration of the solution is determined by adding excess iodine and back-titrating with standard sodium thiosulfate solution. To back-titrate, measure by pipette, 50 ml of the 0.01 N iodine solutions into each of two 500 ml iodine flasks A and B. To flask A (blank) add 25 ml distilled water and into flask B (Sample) measure 25 ml sulphite solution by pipette. Stopper the flasks and allow to react for 5 minutes. Prepare the working sulphite-TCM solution at the same time iodine solution is added to the flasks. By means of a burette containing standardized 0.01 N thiosulfate, titrate each flask in turn to a pale yellow. Then add 5 ml starch solution and continue the titration until the blue color disappears.

Working sulphite – TCM Solution: Measure 2 ml of the standard solution into a 100 ml volumetric flask by pipette and bring to mark with 0.04 M TCM.

10. **Pararosaline stock solution:** Dissolve 0.500 gm of specially purified pararosaniline (PRA) in 100 ml of distilled water and keep for 2 days (48 hours).

Pararosaline working solution: 10 ml of stock PRA is taken in a 250 ml volumetric flask. Add 15 ml conc. HCL and make up to volume with distilled water.

Procedure for Sampling (For 24 hours)

Place 50 ml of TCM in a large impinger and collect the sample 1 LPM. (If high SO_2 concentration is expected, flow rate to be adjusted to 0.5 LPM or less). Determine the total air volume by multiplying the air flow rate by the time in minute. After sample collection (dichlorosulphitomercurate) of sample it is relatively stable. At the temperature of 25° C and above, the loss of SO_2 occurs. Therefore, it is advisable to store the sample at 5° C till the analysis.

Analysis of Samples

After receiving the samples in the laboratory, check the volume of absorbing media and record it. Normally the volume of absorbing reagent is likely to be reduced as a result of evaporation losses. Make up the evaporation loss by adding fresh, boiled cooled distill water. Pipette 10 ml of aliquot from the sample into a 25 ml volumetric flask. Prepare blank solution by measuring 10 ml of unexposed TCM solution into 25 ml volumetric flask. Then add 1 ml sulphamic acid and allow standing for 10 minutes for reaction, and then add 2 ml of formaldehyde and 2 ml of working PRA solution. Mix thoroughly of sample and after 30 minute, set the spectrophotometer at 0.0 absorbance with blank and then take reading of sample at 560 nm on a spectrophotometer.

Calculations:

I. Normality of Thiosulfate solution

The normality of this solution N, is calculated as follows:

$$N = \frac{W \times 10^3 \times 0.1}{V \times 35.67}$$

Where:

V = Volume thiosulfate used, ml

W = Weight of potassium iodate, g

35.67 = Equivalent weight of potassium iodate

II. Concentrations of sulphite solution

The amount of sulphur dioxide per milliliter in the standard solution is calculated as follows:

$$C = \frac{(V_1 - V_2) \times N \times K}{V}$$

Where:

C = SO_2 concentration in µg/ml

V_1 = Volume of thiosulfate for blank, ml

V_2 = Volume of thiosulfate for sample, ml

N = Normality of thiosulfate

K = 3200 (Milli equivalent weight $SO_2/\mu g$)

V = Volume of standard sulphite solution, ml

III. Conversion of volume

Convert the volume of air sampled to the volume at the reference conditions of 25° C 760 mm:

$$V_r = V \times \frac{P}{760} \times \frac{298}{t + 273}$$

Where:

$V_{r =}$ Volume of air at 25° C

V = Volume of air sampled, liters

P = Barometric pressure, mm Hg

t = Temperature of air sampled, °C

IV. The concentration of SO_2 $\mu g/m^3$ in the sample is calculated as follows:

$$SO_2 \mu g/m^3 = \frac{(A - A_o) \times 10^3 \times B}{V}$$

Where:

A = Sample absorbance

A_0 = Reagent blank absorbance

10^3 = Conversion litres to cubic meters

B = Calibration factor, μg/absorbance

V = Volume of air sampled in liters

(c) Respiratory suspended particulate matters (RSPM)

Principle: Ambient air laden with suspended particulate matter passes through a cyclone. The coarse, non-respirable dust is separated from the air stream by centrifugal forces acting on the solid particles. These particles collected in hopper of the cyclone. The fine dust forming the respirable fraction passes through the cyclone and carried by air stream to the 20.3 × 25.5 cm (8 × 10 inch) filter paper at a nominal flow rates from 0.90 to 1.20 cubic meters per minute. Particles within the size range of 10 microns to 0.5 microns are ordinarily collected on glass fiber filters and SPM bigger than 10 microns collected in a separate sampling bottle. The mass concentration of suspended particulates in the ambient air, expressed in microgram per cubic meter, is calculated by measuring the mass of collected particulates and the volume of air sampled.

Requirements:

1. Glass fiber filters (Whatman GF/A)
2. Respiratory dust sampler

Procedure of Sampling

1. Preparation of filters: Expose the filter paper against light source and inspect for pinholes, particulates or other imperfections. The filter paper was dried in oven at 105° C for 1 hour and the equilibrated in desiccator for about one hour, weigh the filter paper.

Pre-use Checks for the Cyclone Assembly

Remove the dust collection bottle at the bottom of the cyclone. Wipe the bottle inside with a clean tissue paper. Use a small paint brush to clear any dust residues at the bottom hole of the cyclone body. If the seal rings are dry, apply a little silicon greas.

2. Procedure of sample collection: following steps were followed during the collection of samples.
3. Open the shelter of respiratory dust sampler (RDS).
4. Mount a preweighed glass fibers filter paper in position with the rough side up and tighten the nuts.
5. Allow the RDS to run for specified length of time (24 hours).
6. During the sampling time, flow rate have taken hourly.
7. At the end of sampling, remove the filter from the mount very carefully. Fold the filter in half upon itself with the collected material enclosed within. Place the filter in a desiccator.
8. Collect the dust from the bin of cyclone and weigh.

Analysis of Samples

In the lab, remove the filter from desiccator and take out the filter paper from the envelope. Dry the filter paper by keeping on watch glass in hot about one hour in hot air oven at 105° C for 1 hour. Equilibrated the exposed filters for about one hour in desiccator, carry the desiccator to the balance and weigh on the analytical balance to the nearest 0.1 milligram.

Calculation

I. Calculation of volume of air sampled

$$V = Q \times T$$

Where:

V = Air sampled (m^3)

Q = Hourly average flow rate (m^3 per minute)

T = Sampling time (minutes)

$$Q = \frac{Q_1 + Q_2}{2}$$

Where:

Q_1 = Initial flow rate

Q_2 = Final flow rate

II. Calculation of mass concentration of respiratory suspended particulate matter (RSPM):

The mass concentration of RSPM calculated as follows:

$$\text{RSPM} (\mu/m^3) = \frac{(Fw - Iw) \times 10^6}{V}$$

Where:

Fw = Final weight of exposed filter paper in grams.

Iw = Initial weight of unexposed filter paper in grams.

V = Air volume sampled in cubic meters.

Concentration of dust (non-respirable particulates) in the dust tight bin of cyclone calculated same as RSPM, after addition of concentration of dust of the filter paper and non-respirable particulates, we can get concentration of total suspended particulate matter.

Calculation methods of the concentration of total dust (SPM) and RSPM are summarized in Annexure.

ANNEXURE

Sample Calcualtion for Respirable particulate matter and total suspended particulate matter using Envirotech Respirable dust sampler APM 460

S.No.	Readings	Readings
A (i)	Initial manometer Reading	——m^3/min
(ii)	Final manometer Reading	——m^3/min
B (i)	Initial filter Paper Weight	—— gm
(ii)	Final filter paper weight	—— gm
C (i)	Initial cyclone cup weight	—— gm
(ii)	Final cyclone cup weight	—— gm
D (i)	Initial time totalizer reading	—— hrs
(ii)	Final time totalizer reading	—— hrs
E	Average flow rate = $\frac{[A(i) + A(ii)]}{2}$	——m^3/min
F	Total on time of machine = D (ii) – D (i) × 60	—— min
G	Respirable dust accumulated on Filter = B (ii) – B (i)	—— gm
H	Non respirable dust accumulated in cyclone cup = C (ii) – C (i)	—— gm
I	Total vome of air passed through cyclone/filter paper = E × F	—— m^3
J	Respirable particulate matter concentration = $\frac{(H) \times 10^6}{(I)}$	—— $\mu g/m^3$
K	(Non respirable particulate matter concentration = $\frac{(G) \times 10^6}{(I)}$	—— $\mu g/m^3$
L	Suspended Particulate matter or total suspended particulate matter = J+K	—— $\mu g/m^3$

Air Quality Index

The Air Quality Index (AQI) is a standardized indicator of the air quality in a given location. It measures mainly ground-level ozone and particulates (except the pollen count), but may also include sulphur dioxide, and nitrogen dioxide. Various agencies around the world measure such indices, though definitions may change between places.

The United States Environmental Protection Agency (EPA) and the Meteorological Service of Canada (MSC) differ on what AQI structure and health classification is used:

Health classifications used by the EPA:

0-50 Good is usually green

51-100 Moderate is usually yellow

101-150 Unhealthy for sensitive groups is usually orange

151-200 Unhealthy is usually red

201-300 Very unhealthy is usually purple

301-500 Hazardous is usually maroon

The EPA's AQI 100 corresponds to 0.08 ppm ozone, and to other levels for other pollutants. Source: EPA

The AQI standards in Canada are notably more protective of health. The current health classifications used by the Meteorological Service of Canada (MSC) are as follows:

0-25*: Good (green)

26*-50: Fair (yellow)

51-100: Poor (orange)

101+: Very poor (red)

In Ontario, 31 is the upper limit for good and 32 the lower limit for moderate. Zero to 15 is classified as very good, and is given the color blue.

Other Indexes

United States

The United States Environment Protection Agency (USEPA) developed the Pollutant Standards Index (PSI) to provide accurate, timely and easily understandable information about daily levels of air pollution.

It is no longer in use, having been replaced by the AQI, which is more sensitive. For example, particulate matter with an aerodynamic diameter less than 2.5 micrometres (PM2.5) is a sub index, replacing the less sensitive PM10 component of the PSI.

United Kingdom

The Met Office of the United Kingdom (UK) issues air quality forecasts wherein the level of pollution is described either as an index (ranging from 1 to 10) or as a banding (low, moderate, high or very high). These levels are based on the health effects of each pollutant.

In June 2007, the EPA proposed a slight possible tightening of the pollution standards associated with smog after an independent EPA scientific board said that the standard "needs to be substantially reduced" and that there is "no scientific justification" for retaining the current, weaker standard

In light of the new scientific findings, one should expect adjustments in the AQI such that pollution currently denoted as "moderate" will in the future be recognized as "unhealthy." The AQI can worsen (go up) due to lack of dilution with fresh air. Stagnant air, often caused by an anticyclone or temperature inversion, or other lack of winds lets air pollution remain in a local area. On these days, the news media may ask the public to carpool or use public transport, or take other air pollution prevention measures such as teleworking.

The forecast is produced for a number of different pollutants and their typical health effects are shown in the following table.

Pollutant Health Effects at High Level

Nitrogen dioxide

Ozone

Sulphur dioxide These gases irritate the airways of the lungs, increasing the symptoms of those suffering from lung diseases.

Index	Banding	Health Effect
1-3	Low	Effects are unlikely to be noticed even by individuals who know they are sensitive to air pollutants.
4-6	Moderate	Mild effects, unlikely to require action, may be noticed amongst sensitive individuals.
7-9	High	Significant effects may be noticed by sensitive individuals and action to avoid or reduce these effects may be needed (e.g. reducing exposure by spending less time in polluted areas outdoors). Asthmatics will find that their 'reliever' inhaler is likely to reverse the effects on the lung.
10	Very High	The effects on sensitive individuals described for 'High' levels of

Particulates

Fine particles can be carried deep into the lungs where they can cause inflammation and a worsening of heart and lung diseases.

Hong Kong

The Air Pollution Index (API) levels for Hong Kong are related to the measured concentrations of ambient respirable suspended particulate (RSP), sulphur dioxide (SO_2), carbon monoxide (CO), ozone (O_3) and nitrogen dioxide (NO_2) over a 24-hour period based on the potential health effects of air pollutants.

An API level at or below 100 means that the pollutant levels are in the satisfactory range over 24 hour period and pose no acute or immediate health effects. However, air pollution consistently at "High" levels (API of 51 to 100) in a year may mean that the annual Hong Kong "Air Quality Objectives" for protecting long-term health effects could be violated. Therefore, chronic health effects may be observed if one is persistently exposed to an API of 51 to 100 for a long time.

"Very High" levels (API in excess of 100) means that levels of one or more pollutant(s) is/are in the unhealthy range. The Hong Kong Environmental Protection Department provides advice to the public regarding precautionary actions to take for such levels.

API	Air Pollution Level	Health Implications
0-25	Low	Not expected.
26-50	Medium	Not expected for the general population.
51-100	High	Acute health effects are not expected but chronic effects may be observed if one is persistently exposed to such levels.
100-200	Very High	People with existing heart or respiratory illnesses may notice mild aggravation of their health conditions. Generally healthy individuals may also notice some discomfort.
201-500	Severe	People with existing heart or respiratory illnesses may experience significant aggravation of their symptoms. There may also be widespread symptoms in the healthy population (e.g. eye irritation, wheezing, coughing, phlegm and sore throats).

Malaysia

The air quality in Malaysia is reported as the API or Air Pollution Index. Four of the index's pollutant components (i.e., carbon monoxide, ozone, nitrogen dioxide and sulfur dioxide) are reported in ppmv but PM10 particulate matter is reported in $\mu g/m^3$.

Unlike the American AQI, the index number can exceed 500. Above 500, a state of emergency is declared in the reporting area. Usually, this means that non-essential government services are suspended, and all ports in the affected area closed. There may also be a prohibition on private sector commercial and industrial activities in the reporting area excluding the food sector.

Singapore

Singapore uses the Pollutant Standards Index to report on its air quality.

Notes

In the context of this article about air quality:

- ppmv = parts per million by volume = volume of pollutant gas per million volumes of ambient air
- PM_{10} = particulate matter smaller than 10 μm in diameter
- $\mu g/m^3$ = micrograms per cubic metre of ambient air
- μm = micrometre

Pollutant Standards Index

The Pollutant Standards Index, or PSI, provides a uniform system of measuring pollution levels for the major air pollutants. It is based on a scale devised by the United States Environmental Protection Agency (USEPA) to provide a way for broadcasts and newspapers to report air quality on a daily basis.

The PSI is reported as a number on a scale of 0 to 500 and is the air quality indicator. These index figures enable the public to determine whether the air pollution levels in a particular location are good, unhealthy, hazardous or worse. The PSI is used in a number of countries including the United States and Singapore. However, since 1999, the United States EPA has replaced the Pollution Standards Index (PSI) with the Air Quality Index (AQI) to incorporate new PM2.5 and ozone standards.

PSI in Singapore

The highest PSI reading on record in Singapore is 226 in September 1997. The PSI chart below is grouped by index values and descriptors, according to the National Environment Agency.

PSI	Descriptor	General Health Effects
0-50	Good	None
51-100	Moderate	Few or none for the general population
101-200	Unhealthy	Mild aggravation of symptoms among susceptible persons i.e. those with underlying conditions such as chronic heart or lung ailments; transient symptoms of irritation e.g. eye irritation, sneezing or coughing in some of the healthy population.
201-300	Very Unhealthy	Moderate aggravation of symptoms and decreased tolerance in persons with heart or lung disease; more widespread symptoms of transient irritation in the healthy population.
301-400	Hazardous	Early onset of certain diseases in addition to significant aggravation of symptoms in susceptible persons; and decreased exercise tolerance in healthy persons.
Above 400	Hazardous	PSI levels above 400 may be life-threatening to ill and elderly persons. Healthy people may experience adverse symptoms that affect normal activity.

Note: This chart reflects those shown in Singapore and may differ for other countries.

Environmental Effects of Air Pollution

Photochemical smog or Log Angles smog

Photochemical smog was first observed in Log Angles in California a new and serious form of air in 1944. It was first characterized by reduced visibility eye irrigation and plant damage (i.e., metallic sheen on leaves) whereas Landon smog is characterized by bronchitis irrigation. It is not related to smoke or fog. It is worst in sunshine and unlike London type of smog which peaks early in the day. It peaks in the afternoon. It also called as photochemical smog as an important reaction, association of NO_2 is caused by sunlight.

The phenomenon of photochemical smog has been observed in major metropolition cities of the world. In India Delhi, Mumbai, Kolkatta, Chennai, Banglore etc are the ideal candidates for the formation of photochemical smog. The condition for the formation of smongare air stagnation, abundant sunlight and high concentration of hydrocarbons and nitrogen oxide in the atmosphere.

Smog arises in lower atmosphere due to photochemical reaction by the interaction of hydrocarbon and nitrogen oxide released by exhaust of automobile and some stationary sources.

Main component of Photochemical smog

The main component of smog are unsaturated hydrocarbon, NO_x, and some sulphur compounds. The various components of Photochemical smog are as below:

(a) Inorganic gases such as O_3, NO_x , hydrogen peroxide and carbon monoxide.

(b) Organic peroxide, organic hydroperoxide and PAN (Peroxy-acyl-nitrate), PBN (Peroxy-benzoyl - nitrate), Peroxy Propyonyl nitrate (PPN), Peracetic acid (CH_3COOOH), acetyl peroxide ($CH_3(CO)OO(CO)CH_3$), ethyl hydroperoxide, n-butylhydroperoxide.

The components along with their level are given in table:

Component	Optimum level (PPM)
CO	2.0
Nitric oxide	0.15
Nitrogen oxide	0.20
Unsaturated Hydrocarbon	0.05
Aromatic compounds	0.20
O_3	0.10
Aldeydes	0.20
Organic Peroxide	0.03

Chemical Reactions in the Formation of Photochemical Smog

In the air the formation of PAN, NOx, O_3, has been indicatives of smog formation. The serious conditions of smog occur when the oxidants level increase 0.15 per hour. Photochemical reactions are initiated by ultraviolet light. PBN is produced in photochemical smog in presence of NO2 and olefins. Hydrocarbons and olefinds are especially conductive of smog formation. PBxN is two times more powerful than PAN.

Photochemical reaction start with the combination of N_2 and O_2. They react at the high temperature level in hydrocarbon combustion flames and form nitric acid. These are primary photochemical product in smog formation.

The important step in smog formation are:

1. Formation of Nitric Oxide (NO):

   $N_2 (g) + O_2 (g) \longrightarrow 2NO$

   NO, reacts further with O_2 and form NO_2

   $2NO + O_2 \longrightarrow 2NO_2$

2. Nitrogten dioxde is a Part of Photolytic NO2 Cycle:

   According to Haagen smit theory, UV rays cause the photo-dissociation of NO_2 to form NO and atomic oxygen.

   $NO_2 \xrightarrow{UV} NO + O$ (Atomic oxygen)

3. Formation of Oxidants

   Formation of O_3, nascent oxygen and peroxide etc. during the smog formation:

   $NO + [O] \longrightarrow NO_2 \quad [0] + O_2 \longrightarrow O_3$

4. Reaction involving oxygen species:

   $O + O_2 + M \longrightarrow O_3 + M$

   Where M is a body such as N_2, O_2 or CO.

5. Combination of O_2 and NO to close the cycle:

   $O_3 + NO \longrightarrow NO_2 + O_2$

   O_3 can also combine NO_2 to form N_2O_5

   $2NO_2 + O_3 \longrightarrow N_2O_5 + O_2$

   Hydrocarbons which emitted form automobiles reacts by free radicals mechanism with [O] or O_3 to form secondary pollutants i.e., aldehyde, ketone and organic peroxide.

6. Production of organic free radical from Hydrocarbon:

   $O + RH \longrightarrow R^{\cdot} +$ other products

Acid Rain

What is Acid Rain?

Acid rain is a widespread term used to describe all forms of acid precipitation (rain, snow, hail, fog, etc.). Atmospheric pollutants, particularly oxides of sulphur and nitrogen, can cause precipitation to become more acidic when converted to sulphuric and nitric acids, hence the term acid rain. Acid deposition, acid rain and acid precipitation all relate to the chemistry of air pollution and moisture in the atmosphere. Acid rain is a result of air pollution. When any type of fuel is burnt, lots of different chemicals are produced. The smoke that comes from a fire or the fumes that come out of a car exhaust don't just contain the sooty grey particles that you can see - they also contains lots of invisible gases that can be even more harmful to our environment.

Power stations, factories and cars all burn fuels and therefore they all produce polluting gases. Some of these gases (especially nitrogen oxides and sulphur dioxide) react with the tiny droplets of water in clouds to form sulphuric and nitric acids. The rain from these clouds then falls as very weak acid - which is why it is known as "acid rain".

How acidic is acid rain?

Acidity is measured using a scale called the pH scale. This scale goes from 0 to 14. 0 is the most acidic and 14 is the most alkaline (opposite of acidic). Something with a pH value of 7, we call neutral, this means that it is neither acidic nor alkaline. Very strong acids will burn if they touch your skin and can even destroy metals. Acid rain is much, much weaker than this, never acidic enough to burn your skin. Rain is always slightly acidic because it mixes with naturally occurring oxides in the air. Unpolluted rain would have a pH value of between 5 and 6. When the air becomes more polluted with nitrogen oxides and sulphur dioxide the acidity can increase to a pH value of 4. Some rain has even been recorded as being pH2. Vinegar has a pH value of 2.2 and lemon juice has a value of pH 2.3. Even the strongest recorded acid rain is only about as acidic as lemon juice or vinegar and we know that these don't harm us - so why do we worry about acid rain?

Air Pollutant	% that mobile sources contribute to acid rain	% that other sources contribute to acid rain
Volatile organic compound	37%	63%
Nitrogen oxide	49%	51%
Carbon monoxide	81%	19%
Particulate matter	27%	73%

The Effects of Acid Rain

Acid rain can be carried great distances in the atmosphere, not just between countries but also from continent to continent. The acid can also take the form of snow, mists and dry dusts. The rain sometimes falls many miles from the source of pollution but wherever it falls it can have a serious effect on soil, trees, buildings and water. Forests all over the world are dying, fish are dying. In Scandinavia there are dead lakes, which are crystal clear and contain no living creatures or plant life. Many of Britain's freshwater fish are threatened; there have been reports of deformed fish being hatched. This leads to fish-eating birds and animals being affected also. Is acid rain responsible for all this? Scientists have been doing a lot of research into how acid rain affects the environment.

Forests

It is thought that acid rain can cause trees to grow more slowly or even to die but scientists have found that it is not the only cause. The same amount of acid rain seems to have more effect in some areas than it does in others. As acid rain falls on a forest it trickles through the leaves of the trees and runs down into the soil below. Some of it finds its way into streams and then on into rivers and lakes. Some types of soil can help to neutralise the acid - they have what is called a "buffering capacity".

Other soils are already slightly acidic and these are particularly susceptible to the effects of acid rain. Acid rain can effect trees in several different ways, it may:

- Dissolve and wash away the nutrients and minerals in the soil which help the trees to grow.
- Cause the release of harmful substances such as aluminium into the soil.
- Wear away the waxy protective coating of leaves, damaging them and preventing them from being able to photosynthesise properly.

A combination of these effects weakens the trees which means that they can be more easily attacked by diseases and insects or injured by bad weather. It is not just trees that are affected by acid rain, other plants may also suffer.

Lakes and Rivers

It is in aquatic habitats that the effects of acid rain are most obvious. Acid rain runs off the land and ends up in streams, lakes and marshes - the rain also falls directly on these areas.

As the acidity of a lake increases, the water becomes clearer and the numbers of fish and other water animals decline. Some species of plant and animal are better able to survive in acidic water than others. Freshwater shrimps, snails, mussels are the most quickly affected by acidification followed by fish such as minnows, salmon and roach. The roe and fry (eggs and young) of the fish are the worst affected, the acidity of the water can cause deformity in young fish and can prevent eggs from hatching properly.

The acidity of the water does not just affect species directly, it also causes toxic substances like aluminium to be released into the water from the soil, harming fish and other aquatic animals. Lakes, rivers and marshes each have their own fragile ecosystem with many different species of plants and animals all depending on one another to survive. If a species of fish disappears, the animals which feed on it will gradually disappear too. If the extinct fish used to feed on a particular species of large insect, that insect population will start to grow, this in turn will affect the smaller insects or plankton on which the larger insect feeds.

Buildings

Every type of material will become eroded sooner or later by the effects of the climate. Water, wind, ice and snow all help in the erosion process but unfortunately, acid rain can help to make this natural process even quicker. Statues, buildings, vehicles, pipes and cables can all suffer. The worst affected are things made from limestone or sandstone as these types of rock are particularly susceptible and can be affected by air pollution in gaseous form as well as by acid rain.

Where is it coming from?

Until relatively recently air pollution has been seen as a local issue. It was in southern Scandinavia in the late 1950's that the problems of acid rain were first observed and it was then that people began to realise that the origins of this pollution were far away in Britain and Northern Europe. One early answer to industrial air pollution was to build very tall chimneys. Unfortunately all this does is push the polluting gases up into the clouds allowing emissions to float away on the wind. The wind carries the pollution many hundreds of miles away where it eventually falls as acid rain. In this way Britain has contributed at least 16% of the acid deposition in Norway. Over ninety percent of Norway's acid pollution comes from other countries. The worst European polluters are Germany, UK, Poland and Spain, each of them producing over a million tons of sulphur emissions in 1994. Governments are now beginning to admit that acid rain is a serious environmental problem and many countries are now taking steps to reduce the amount of sulphur and nitrogen emissions.

What can be done?

Reduce emissions:

- Burning fossil fuels is still one of the cheapest ways to produce electricity so people are now researching new ways to burn fuel which don't produce so much pollution.
- Governments need to spend more money on pollution control even if it does mean an increase in the price of electricity.

- Sulphur can also be 'washed' out of smoke by spraying a mixture of water and powdered limestone into the smokestack.
- Cars are now fitted with catalytic converters which remove three dangerous chemicals from exhaust gases.

Find alternative sources of energy

- Governments need to invest in researching different ways to produce energy.
- Two other sources that are currently used are hydroelectric and nuclear power. These are 'clean' as far as acid rain goes but what other impact do they have on our environment?
- Other sources could be solar energy or windmills but how reliable would these be in places where it is not very windy or sunny?
- All energy sources have different benefits and costs and all theses have to be weighed up before any government decides which of them it is going to use.

Conserving Resources

- Greater subsidies of public transport by the government to encourage people to use public transport rather than always travelling by car.
- Every individual can make an effort to save energy by switching off lights when they are not being used and using energy-saving appliances - when less electricity is being used, pollution from power plants decreases.
- Walking, cycling and sharing cars all reduce the pollution from vehicles.

Restoring the Damage done by Acid Rain

Lakes and rivers can have powdered limestone added to them to neutralise the water - this is called "liming". Liming, however, is expensive and its effects are only temporary - it needs to be continued until the acid rain stops. The people of Norway and Sweden have successfully used liming to help restore lakes and streams in their countries. A major liming programme is currently taking place in Wales.

Air Quality in Asian Cities

1. Air pollution continues to pose a significant threat to the environment, quality of life and health of the urban population in Asia. Many Asian cities have developed some form of air quality management (AQM) system to address the increasing levels of urban air pollution. However, the sophistication and completeness of the AQM system may not be adequate to effectively address the air pollution problem.
2. An ongoing study1 by the Clean Air Initiative for Asian Cities, summarizing air quality data from 20 cities in Asia for the period 1993 to 2004 shows that, on average, there has been a moderate to slight decrease in pollution levels for sulfur dioxide (SO_2), total suspended particulate matter (SPM), and fine particulates, also known as PM10. Although particulate matter remains at levels harmful to human health, SO_2 levels are now, on average, below the guideline values set by the World Health Organization – proving that air quality management policies and measures can work in Asia. Ambient concentrations of NO_2 are seen to remain at gradually increasing levels and just above the WHO guidelines. These air quality data collected by CAI-Asia from various government agencies and other sources have been validated by the appropriate government agency in each city.
3. A macro-analysis of air pollution trends in twenty Asian cities shows that, in general, TSP and PM10 have decreased from 1993 to 2004, but ambient levels remain above limits set by the World Health Organization (WHO), US Environmental Protection Agency and the WHO - European

   The aggregated data for SO_2 clearly shows that this problem have been sufficiently dealt with by most Asian cities considering that the levels in the recent years fall within WHO guidelines. The aggregated data for NO_2 shows that the levels have been stabilized around WHO guideline of 40µg/m^3, withstanding the continued increase in motorization especially of two and three wheelers in the region.

4. In 2000, the WHO_2 abandoned the standards for particulates because time-series Epidemiological studies then were unable to define a threshold below which no health effects occur; even at low levels of particulate matter, short-term exposure is associated with health effects. Ambient concentrations of PM10 were then compared with limits set by USEPA (50µg/m^3). In the 2005 update 3 of the WHO air quality guidelines, however, the WHO has indicated an annual PM10 guideline of 20µg/m^3 since this is the lowest level at which total, cardiopulmonary and lung cancer mortality has been shown to increase.
5. An analysis of the levels of ambient concentrations of pollutants on a per city basis, indicate that particulate matter (TSP and PM10) are main pollutants of concern for most of the cities. PM10 average for 2000-2004 is lowest in Singapore at 30µg/m^3, meeting the 50µg/m^3 standards set by USEPA (Singapore adopts USEPA standards). This value, however, will fail now when compared with the WHO 2005 updated guideline. All recent levels of PM10 in the 20 cities in the study then, fail to meet WHO standards.
6. All of the eighteen cities with SO_2 data, except for Beijing, meet the WHO guidelines confirming the overall average trend (Figure 9.1) that SO_2 has been sufficiently dealt with by Asian cities.
7. Seventeen out of the twenty cities in the study have NO_2 data, eight of which (47%) meet the WHO guideline while the remaining nine cities (53%) exceeding the 40µg/m^3 guideline. This may indicate that NO_2 is an emerging pollutant of concern for Asia.

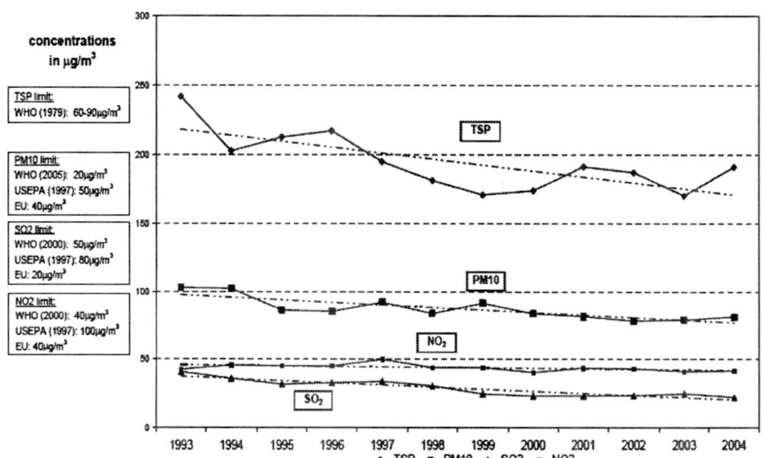

Fig. 9.1: Trends of Major Criteria Air Pollutants (1993-2004)

[1]CAI-Asia, in cooperation with the UNEP and WHO supported project, Air Pollution in the Major and Mega-cities of Asia, is conducting the 2nd Stage of the Benchmarking Study on Air Quality Management, Capability of selected Asian cities. Cities included in the study: Bangkok, Beijing, Busan, Colombo, Dhaka, Delhi, Hanoi, Ho Chi Minh, Hong Kong, Jakarta, Kathmandu, Kolkata, Mumbai, Manila, Seoul, Shanghai, Singapore, Surabaya, Taipei and Tokyo

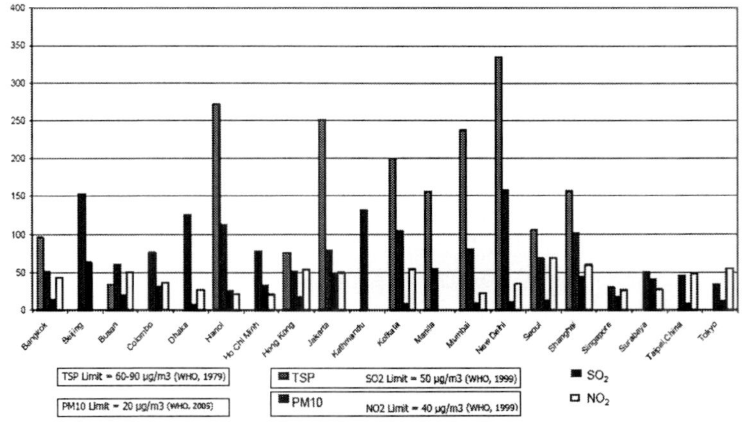

Fig. 9.2: Average Annual Air Pollution Concentrations (2000-2004) in Selected Asian Cities

[2]WHO, 1999. World Health Organization Guidelines for Air Quality, Geneva, 2000

[3]WHO, 2005. WHO Air Quality Guidelines Global Update 2005. Report on a Working Group Meeting, Bonn Germany. 18-20 October 2005

Table 9.1: Major air pollutants and their associated health hazards

Name of pollutant	Health impacts
RSPM	Respiratory illness, including chronic bronchitis and asthma; heart diseases.
SO_2	Heart diseases; respiratory problems including pulmonary emphysema, cancer, eye burning, headache, etc.
NO_2	Lung irritation, viral infection, airway resistance, chest tightness, etc.
SPM	Pneumoconiosis, restrictive lung diseases, asthma, cancer, etc.
Benzene	It causes immunotoxicity, carcinogenicity, asthma, anemia, unconsciousness etc.
Ozone	Impaired lung function, chest pains, coughing, irritation of eyes, nose etc.
CO	CO poisoning cause cherry lips, unconsciousness, death by asphyxiation etc.
Lead	It causes decreased hemoglobin synthesis, anemia, damage the nervous and renal (kidney) systems etc.

The Kyoto Protocol - A Brief Summary

The Kyoto Protocol to the United Nations Framework Convention on Climate Change strengthens the international response to climate change. Adopted by consensus at the third session of the Conference of the Parties (COP_3) in December 1997, it contains legally binding emissions targets for Annex I (developed) countries for the post-2000 period.

By arresting and reversing the upward trend in greenhouse gas emissions that started in these countries 150 years ago, the Protocol promises to move the international community one step closer to achieving the Convention's ultimate objective of preventing "dangerous anthropogenic [man-made] interference with the climate system".

The developed countries commit themselves to reducing their collective emissions of six key greenhouse gases by at least 5%. This group target will be achieved through cuts of 8% by Switzerland, most Central and East European states, and the European Union (the EU will meet its target by distributing different rates among its member states); 7% by the US; and 6% by Canada, Hungary, Japan, and Poland. Russia, New Zealand, and Ukraine are to stabilize their emissions, while Norway may increase emissions by up to 1%, Australia by up to 8%, and Iceland 10%. The six gases are to be combined in a "basket", with reductions in individual gases translated into "CO_2 equivalents" that are then added up to produce a single figure.

Each country's emissions target must be achieved by the period 2008-2012. It will be calculated as an average over the five years. "Demonstrable progress" towards meeting the target must be made by 2005. Cuts in the three most important gases – carbon dioxide (CO_2), methane (CH_4), and nitrous oxide (N_20) - will be measured against a base year of 1990 (with exceptions for some countries with economies in transition).

Cuts in three long-lived industrial gases – hydrofluorocarbons (HFCs), perfluorocarbons (PFCs), and sulphur hexafluoride (SF_6) - can be measured against either a 1990 or 1995 baseline. (A major group of industrial gases, chlorofluorocarbons, or CFCs, are dealt with under the 1987 Montreal Protocol on Substances that Deplete the Ozone Layer.)

Actual emission reductions will be much larger than 5%. Compared with emissions levels projected for the year 2000, the richest industrialized countries (OECD members) will need to reduce their collective output by about 10%. This is because many of these countries will not succeed in meeting their earlier non-binding aim of returning emissions to 1990 levels by the year 2000; their emissions have in fact risen since 1990. While the countries with economies in transition have experienced falling emissions since 1990, this trend is now reversing.

Therefore, for the developed countries as a whole, the 5% Protocol target represents an actual cut of around 20% when compared with the emissions levels that are projected for 2010 if no emissions-control measures are adopted.

Countries will have a certain degree of flexibility in how they make and measure their emissions reductions. In particular, an international "emissions trading" regime will be established allowing industrialized countries to buy and sell emissions credits amongst themselves. They will also be able to acquire "emission reduction units" by financing certain kinds of projects in other developed countries through a mechanism known as Joint Implementation. In addition, a "Clean Development Mechanism" for promoting sustainable development will enable industrialized countries to finance emissions-reduction projects in developing countries and receive credit for doing so. The operational guidelines for these various schemes are being elaborated under a two-year Plan of Action that is to conclude at COP6.

They will pursue emissions cuts in a wide range of economic sectors. The Protocol encourages governments to cooperate with one another, improve energy efficiency, reform the energy and transportation sectors, promote renewable forms of energy, phase out inappropriate fiscal measures and market imperfections, limit methane emissions from waste management and energy systems, and protect forests and other carbon "sinks".

The measurement of changes in net emissions (calculated as emissions minus removals of CO_2) from forests is methodologically complex and still needs to be clarified.

The Protocol will advance the implementation of existing commitments by all countries. Under the Convention, both developed and developing countries agree to take measures to limit emissions and promote adaptation to future climate change impacts; submit information on their national climate change programmes and inventories; promote technology transfer; cooperate on scientific and technical research; and promote public awareness, education, and training. The Protocol also reiterates the need to provide "new and additional" financial resources to meet the "agreed full costs" incurred by developing countries in carrying out these commitments.

The Conference of the Parties (COP) of the Convention will also serve as the meeting of the Parties (MOP) for the Protocol. This structure is expected to reduce costs and facilitate the management of the intergovernmental process. Parties to the Convention that are not Parties to the Protocol will be able to participate in Protocol-related meetings as observers.

The new agreement will be periodically reviewed. The Parties will take "appropriate action" on the basis of the best available scientific, technical, and socio-economic information. The first review will take place at the second COP session serving the Protocol. Talks on commitments for the post-2012 period must start by 2005.

The Protocol was opened for signature for one year starting 16 March 1998. It will enter into force 90 days after it has been ratified by at least 55 Parties to the Convention, including developed countries representing at least 55% of the total 1990 carbon dioxide emissions from this group. In the meantime, governments continue to carry out their commitments under the Climate Change Convention. In line with a Plan of Action agreed at the fourth COP in Buenos Aires in November 1998, they are working on many practical issues relating to the Protocol and its future implementation at their regular COP and subsidiary body meetings.

The EU and its Member States ratified the Kyoto Protocol in late May 2002, fulfilling the Commission's ambition to enable the Kyoto Protocol to come into force before the World Summit on Sustainable Development which took place in Johannesburg between 24 August and 4 September 2002.

Climate Change

Climate change is one of the greatest environmental, social and economic threats facing the planet. The warming of the climate system is unequivocal, as is now evident from observations of increases in global average air and ocean temperatures, widespread melting of snow and ice, and rising global mean sea level. The Earth's average surface temperature has risen by 0.76° C since 1850. Most of the warming that has occurred over the last 50 years is very likely to have been caused by human activities. In its Fourth Assessment Report (AR4), published on 2 February 2007, the Intergovernmental Panel on Climate Change (IPCC) projects that, without further action to reduce greenhouse gas emissions, the global average surface temperature is likely to rise by a further 1.8-4.0° C this century. Even the lower end of this range would take the temperature increase since pre-industrial times above 2° C, the threshold beyond which irreversible and possibly catastrophic changes become far more likely.

Projected global warming this century is likely to trigger serious consequences for humanity and other life forms, including a rise in sea levels of between 18 and 59 cm which will endanger coastal areas and small islands, and a greater frequency and severity of extreme weather events.

Human activities that contribute to climate change include in particular the burning of fossil fuels, agriculture and land-use changes like deforestation. These cause emissions of carbon dioxide (CO_2), the main gas responsible for climate change, as well as of other 'greenhouse' gases. To bring climate change to a halt, global greenhouse gas emissions must be reduced significantly.

The European Union is at the forefront of international efforts to combat climate change and has played a key role in the development of the two major treaties addressing the issue, the 1992 United Nations Framework Convention on Climate Change and its Kyoto Protocol, agreed in 1997.

The EU has been taking serious steps to address its own greenhouse gas emissions since the early 1990s. In March 2000 the Commission launched the European Climate Change Programme (ECCP). The ECCP has led to the adoption of a wide range of new policies and measures. Among these is the pioneering EU Emissions Trading Scheme, launched on 1 January 2005, which has become the cornerstone of EU efforts to reduce emissions cost-effectively.

Monitoring data and projections indicate that the 15 European Union members at the time of the EU's ratification of the Kyoto Protocol in 2002 (EU-15) will reach their Kyoto Protocol target for cutting greenhouse gas emissions. This requires emissions in 2008-2012 to be 8% below 1990 levels.

However, Kyoto is only a first step. Ambitious action to reduce global emissions is needed after 2012, when Kyoto's targets expire, in order to limit global warming to 2° C. In January 2007 the European Commission set out proposals and options for achieving this in its Communication "Limiting Global Climate Change to 2 degrees Celsius: The way ahead for 2020 and beyond" The key targets in the Communication, as well as the broad thrust of the integrated energy and climate change strategy of which it forms part, were endorsed by EU leaders at their summit in Brussels on 8-9 March 2007.

The IPCC's latest scientific assessment "Climate Change 2007" can be downloaded here (pdf 1,26MB). Working Group I of the Intergovernmental Panel on Climate Change (IPCC) finalised the Summary for Policymakers of the first volume of "Climate Change 2007", also known as the Fourth Assessment Report (AR4). The report "Climate Change 2007: The Physical Science Basis", assesses the current scientific knowledge of the natural and human drivers of climate change, observed changes in climate, the ability of science to attribute changes to different causes, and projections for future climate change.

Automobile Emissions and Air Pollution

The automotive industry practically dominates the country, through providing one-sixth of its jobs and allowing the transportation that runs life. Americans have become so dependent on automobiles that any indication of necessary change in the industry is met with harsh denial and opposition.

Over the past several decades, the truths about air pollution that results from automobiles have become more and more apparent, and the need for change has become greater. Now, on the brink of futuristic "hybrid" and "ZEV" cars entering the market, change seems to be both practical and profitable. And no matter how America's dependency deals with the problems, we are gaining much greater knowledge and understanding of the possibilities for decreasing the emission of harmful pollutants.

Emissions

The problems inherent to automobile transportation stem from the use of gasoline for power. The burning of cheap, ordinary gasoline gives off primarily three pollutants: hydrocarbons (HC), carbon monoxide (CO), and nitrogen oxides (NO). These products contribute greatly to smog, ozone, cancer, lung disease, illness, and the greenhouse effect. In cities such as Los Angeles, California, the problem is extremely apparent as the city is covered in smog much of the time. Ozone, carbon monoxide, and nitrogen oxides all take away from people's health through destroying tissue, inducing breathing problems, and sometimes leading to cancer.

While the dangers of air pollution are clear still, the industries have been making significant improvements compared to the 1960s, when no attempt was made to limit automotive air pollution. The number of automobiles on the road is increasing by the year. And still, hydrocarbon emissions are down almost 98% from 1960s levels, while carbon monoxide levels are down 96% and nitrogen oxides are down 90%. Smog and air quality levels are changing for the better in major cities. The pollution from automobiles is actually coming from only a small group of "grossly polluting", newer cars, however, as about 10% of cars on the road are accounting for 50% of all harmful emissions put out by automobiles. Studies and analysis shows that, in fact, automobiles are becoming less of the major contributor to air pollution. Instead, other fuel-driven, stationary systems— including factories and oil refineries- are becoming the predominate contributors to harmful emissions. The extremely high emissions levels of airplanes and airports are also gaining concern, as in airports like the Los Angeles International Airport (LAX) where airplane-produced emissions are one of the largest sources of smog in the entire city. Questions also arise about the emissions produced by such accessories as air conditioners within cars, and how one can discern where the problem is truly located and should be corrected. While there still remains a clear problem with automobile-produced emissions into the air, the efforts for change will be cheaper and more effective if directed toward the other harmful, emission-producing systems.

Indoor Air Quality

Indoor Air Quality (IAQ) deals with the content of interior air that could affect health and comfort of building occupants. The IAQ may be compromised by microbial contaminants (mold, bacteria), chemicals (such as carbon monoxide, radon), allergens, or any mass or energy stressor that can induce health effects. Recent findings have demonstrated that indoor air is often more polluted than outdoor air (albeit with different pollutants) although this has not changed the common understanding of air pollution. In fact, indoor air is often a greater health hazard than the corresponding outdoor setting. Using ventilation to dilute contaminants, filtration, and source control are the primary methods for improving indoor air quality in most buildings.

Techniques for analyzing IAQ include collection of air samples, collection of samples on building surfaces and computer modelling of air flow inside buildings. The resulting samples can be analyzed for mold, bacteria, chemicals or other stressors. These investigations can lead to an understanding of the sources of the contaminants and ultimately to strategies for removing the unwanted elements from the air.

Risk Assessment

Radon is the invisible, radioactive atomic gas that results from radioactive decay of some forms of uranium that may be found in rock formations beneath buildings or in certain building materials themselves. Radon is probably the most pervasive serious hazard for indoor air in the United States and Europe, probably responsible for tens of thousands of lung cancer deaths per annum. There are relatively simple tests for radon gas, but these tests are not commonly done, even in areas of known systematic hazards. Radon is a very heavy gas and thus will tend to accumulate at the floor level. Building materials can actually be a significant source of radon, but very little testing is done for stone, rock or tile products brought into building sites. The half life for radon is 3.8 days indicating that once the source is removed, the hazard will be greatly reduced within a few weeks.

Molds and other Allergens

These biological agents can arise from a host of means, but there are two common classes: (a) moisture induced growth of mold colonies and (b) natural substances released into the air such as animal dander and plant pollen. Moisture buildup inside buildings may arise from water penetrating compromised areas of the building envelope or skin, from plumbing leaks, from condensation due to improper ventilation, or from ground moisture penetrating a building slab. In areas where cellulosic materials (paper and wood, including drywall) become moist and fail to dry within 48 hours, mold colonies can propagate and release allergenic spores into the air.

In many cases, if materials have failed to dry out several days after the suspected water event, mold growth is suspected within wall cavities even if it is not immediately visible. Through a mold investigation, which may include destructive inspection, one should be able to determine the presence or absence of mold. In a situation where there is visible mold and the indoor air quality may have been compromised, a mold remediation may be needed. Indoors, mold growth can be inhibited by keeping humidity levels below fifty percent and by eliminating leaks or moisture condensation and accumulation.

There are some varieties of mold that contain toxic compounds (mycotoxins). However, exposure to hazardous levels of mycotoxin via inhalation is not possible in most cases, as toxins are produced by the fungal body and are not at significant levels in the released spores. The primary hazard of mold growth, as it relates to indoor air quality, comes from the allergenic properties of the spore cell wall. More serious than most allergenic properties is the ability of mold to trigger episodes in persons that already have asthma, a serious respiratory disease.

Carbon Monoxide

One of the most acutely toxic indoor air contaminants is carbon monoxide (CO), a colorless, odorless gas that is a byproduct of incomplete combustion of fossil fuels. Common sources of carbon monoxide are tobacco smoke, space heaters using fossil fuels, defective central heating furnaces and automobile exhaust. Improvements in indoor levels of CO are systematically improving from increasing numbers of smoke-free restaurants and other legislated non-smoking buildings. By depriving the brain of oxygen, high levels of carbon monoxide can lead to nausea, unconsciousness and death.

Legionella

Legionellosis or Legionnaire's Disease is caused by a waterborne bacterium that grows best in slow moving or still warm water. The primary route of exposure is aerosolization, most commonly from evaporative cooling towers or showerheads. A common source of Legionella in commercial buildings is from poorly placed or maintained evaporative cooling towers, which often release aerosolized water that may enter nearby ventilation intakes. Outbreaks in medical facilities and nursing homes, where patients are immuno-suppressed and immuno-weak, are the most commonly reported cases of Legionellosis. More than one case has involved outdoor fountains in public attractions. The presence of Legionella in commercial building water supplies is highly under-reported, as healthy people require heavy exposure to acquire infection.

Legionella testing typically involves collecting water samples and surface swabs from evaporative cooling basins, shower heads, faucets, and other locations where warm water collects. The samples are then cultured and colony forming units (cfu) of Legionella are quantified as cfu/Liter.

Legionella is a parasite of protazoans such as amoeba, and thus requires conditions suitable for both organisms. The bacterium forms a biofilm which is resistant to chemical and antimicrobial treatments, including chlorine. Remediation for Legionella outbreaks in commercial buildings vary, but often include very hot water flushes (160°F), sterilization of standing water in evaporative cooling basins, replacement of shower heads, and in some cases flushes of heavy metal salts. Preventative measures include adjusting normal hot water levels to allow for 120°F at the tap, evaluating facility design layout, removing faucet aerators, and periodic testing in suspect areas.

Asbestos Fibers

The U.S. Federal Government (www.osha.gov) and some States have set standards for acceptable levels of asbestos fibers in indoor air. Many common building materials used before 1975 contain asbestos, such as some floor tiles, ceiling tiles, taping muds, pipe wrap, mastics and other insulation materials. Normally significant releases of asbestos fiber do not occur unless the building materials are disturbed, such as by cutting, sanding, drilling or building remodelling. There are particularly stringent regulations applicable to schools. Inhalation of asbestos fibers over long exposure times is associated with increased incidence of lung cancer. While smokers have a greater risk of lung cancer than asbestos workers that do not smoke, smokers that are exposed to high levels of asbestos over many years have a much greater risk of developing lung cancer than either smokers that have not been exposed to asbestos, or persons that have been exposed to high levels of asbestos that do not smoke.

Carbon Dioxide

Carbon dioxide is a surrogate for indoor pollutants emitted by humans and correlates with human metabolic activity. Carbon dioxide at levels that are unusually high indoors may cause occupants to grow drowsy, get headaches, or function at lower activity levels. Humans are the main indoor source of carbon dioxide. Indoor levels are an indicator of the adequacy of outdoor air ventilation relative to indoor occupant density and metabolic activity. To eliminate most Indoor Air Quality complaints, total indoor carbon dioxide should be reduced to below 600 ppm above outdoor levels. NIOSH considers that indoor air concentrations of carbon dioxide that exceed 1,000 ppm are a marker suggesting inadequate ventilation (1,000 ppm equals 0.1%). ASHRAE recommends that carbon dioxide levels not exceed 700 ppm above outdoor ambient levels. The UK standards for schools say that carbon dioxide in all teaching and learning spaces, when measured at seated head height and averaged over the whole day should not exceed 1,500 ppm. The whole day refers to normal school hours (i.e. 9.00am to 3.30pm) and includes unoccupied periods such as lunch breaks. Canadian standards limit carbon dioxide to 3500 ppm. OSHA limits carbon dioxide concentration in the workplace to 5,000 ppm for prolonged periods, and 35,000 ppm for 15 minutes.

How to Improve Indoor Air Quality

According to the National Safety Council, Americans spend about 90 percent of their time indoors, and 65 percent of that time at home. Thus poor indoor air quality can have a significant impact on people's lives, especially those who are most vulnerable: infants and children, pregnant women, the elderly, and those who have chronic illnesses.

Steps can be taken to help improve indoor air quality at home, the workplace, and in other indoor environments. Some of those steps include the following:

Understand the role of Green Cleaning. Many "green" cleaning products contain chemicals that react with ozone to form toxic and irritating chemicals, as described above, through indoor air chemical reactions. The result is air that may contain more hazardous chemicals than were present before the green cleaning products were used. In particular, citrus based solvents and pine-based solvents have been shown to react with ozone and form formaldehyde, higher molecular weight aldehydes, acidic aerosols, and fine and ultrafine particles. Ozone can be removed from outdoor air by filtration with carbon, but large amounts of carbon are required to remove a high fraction of the ozone present in most urban and many ex-urban areas.

Install an air purifier, or an air purification system. Caution is advised. Ozone-based air cleaners are not advised and both the U.S. EPA and the California Air Resources Board have issued advisories on the use of ozone air cleaners. California is currently proposing to regulate ozone air cleaners.

Introducing plants to reduce the levels of indoor air pollution is only minimally effective. Many advocates of plants have advised introducing "toxin-consuming plants" to your home, office, and other indoor environments. Certain plants, including philodendron, spider plants, golden pothos, peace lilies, bamboo palms, mums, and english ivy remove dangerous toxins (e.g., formaldehyde, carbon monoxide, benzene, and others) from the air, but at extremely low rates. Even minimal ventilation with outdoor air removes them more quickly. In fact, the plants themselves do not play a major role in the removal of pollutants whereas the soil or other medium in which they are planted have been shown to play the removal role. The amount of pollutants removed by plants is actually minuscule compared to the removal that occurs even with very low rates of outdoor air ventilation. There is also a risk of increasing indoor humidity levels and of promoting mold growth when indoor plants are not properly maintained. See the article "Can house plants clean indoor air? at [Can_House_Plants_Solve_IAQ_Problems?

Use natural household cleaning products and reduce exposure to potentially toxic airborne substances. Be wary of so-called "green" cleaning products if outdoor ozone concentrations are above 50 ppb.

Use natural pest control techniques indoors whenever possible. Banish pesticides from your garden and lawn as well, as these toxins can easily be transported into the house on shoes and clothing and by air.

Keep your plumbing traps filled with water to help prevent sewer gas from entering the building.

Regularly clean the vents in your kitchen, bathroom, and dryer, and make sure they operate properly.

Do not smoke or allow smoking in your home, and avoid indoor areas where smoking takes place.

Avoid or reduce biological contaminants by maintaining humidifiers, dehumidifiers, and air conditioners; emptying water trays in dehumidifiers, air conditioners, and refrigerators frequently; drying or removing any water-damaged carpets or furniture; and routinely cleaning bedding and items used by pets.

Prevent carbon monoxide exposure by keeping gas appliances properly serviced, having your central heating system inspected and cleaned yearly, and never idling your car inside an attached garage. Install an automatic door closer on the door connecting the garage to the house.

Change filters on central cooling and heating systems and air cleaners according to the manufacturer's directions.

Test your home for radon. Radon can seep into the house from contaminated earth and rock under the home, or from well water and/or building materials. Easy, do-it-yourself kits can be purchased at hardware and other retail outlets.

Ensure Good Ventilation

Have any air-contioning systems inspected regularly to verify that there is no internal contamination build up contributing to poor indoor air quality.

Institutional Roles

The topic of IAQ has become popular due to the greater awareness of health problems caused by mold and triggers to asthma and allergies. Awareness has also been increased by the involvement of the United States Environmental Protection Agency. They have developed an "IAQ Tools for Schools" program to help improve the indoor environmental conditions in educational institutions.

A variety of scientists work in the field of indoor air quality including chemists, physicists, mechanical engineers, biologists, bacteriologists and computer scientists. Some of these professionals are certified by organizations such as the American Industrial Hygiene Association and the American Indoor Air Quality Council. AIHA and A2LA both offer laboratory accreditation programs that relate to indoor air quality.

On the international level, the International Society of Indoor Air Quality and Climate (ISIAQ), formed in 1991, organizes two major conferences, the Indoor Air and the Healthy Buildings series. The next conference, Indoor Air 2008, will take place in Copenhagen, Denmark. Healthy Buildings 2009 will be held in Syracuse, New York. ISIAQ's journal Indoor Air is published 6 times a year and contains peer-reviewed scientific papers with an emphasis on interdisciplinary studies including exposure measurements, modeling, and health.

Indoor Air Pollution in Developing Nations

Indoor air pollution in developing nations is a significant form of indoor air pollution (IAP) that is little known to those in the developed world.

Three billion people in developing nations across the globe rely on biomass, in the form of wood, charcoal, dung, and crop residue, as their domestic cooking fuel. Because much of the cooking is carried out indoors in environments that lack proper ventilation, millions of people, primarily poor women and children face serious health risks. Conservative estimates indicate that between 1.5 and 2 million deaths were attributed to exposure to IAP in developing countries in 2000. Estimates further suggest that approximately 80% of total global exposure to airborne particulate matter occurs indoors in developing nations.

Even though the rate of dependence on biomass fuel is declining, this dwindling resource will not keep up with population growth which could ultimately put environments at even greater risk. In Kenya, efforts are currently being made to address the overall health risks to rural women and children.

Health Implications

Rural Kenya has been the site of various applied research projects to determine the intensity of emissions that commonly occur from use of biomass fuels, particularly wood, dung, and crop residue. Smoke is the result of the incomplete combustion of solid fuel which women and children are exposed to up to seven hours each day in closed environments. These emissions vary from day to day, season to season and with changes in the amount of airflow within the residence. Exposure in poor homes far exceeds accepted safety levels by as much as one hundred times over. Because many Kenyan women utilize a three-stone fire, the worst offender, one kilogram of burning wood produces tiny particles of soot which can clog and irritate the bronchial pathways. The smoke also contains various poisonous gases such as aldehydes, benzene, and carbon monoxide. Exposure to IAP from combustion of solid fuels has been implicated, with varying degrees of evidence, as a causal agent of several diseases. Acute lower respiratory infections (ALRI) and chronic obstructive pulmonary disease (COPD) are the leading causes of disease and death from exposure to smoke. Cataracts and blindness, lung cancer, tuberculosis, premature births and low birth weight are also suspected of being caused by IAP.

Women and primarily girls spend excess time each day in collecting fuel-wood in Kenya which exposes them to even further hazards including vulnerability to rape and also fractures from the weight of carrying heavy loads. This time could be spent in more productive ways such as attending school or income production. The use of biomass coupled with inefficient cooking apparatus leads to a web of social and environmental concerns which directly links to the United Nations Millennium Development Goals.

Interventions

Early Interventions

Unfortunately, finding an affordable solution to address the many effects of IAP – improving combustion, reducing smoke exposure, improving safety and reducing labor, reducing fuel costs, and addressing sustainability – is complex and in need of continual improvement. Efforts to improve cook stoves in the past, beginning in the 1950's, were primarily aimed at minimizing deforestation with no concern for IAP, though the effectiveness of these efforts to save firewood is debatable. Various attempts had various outcomes. For example, some improved stove designs in Kenya significantly reduced particulate emissions but produced higher CO_2 and SO_2 emissions. Flues to remove smoke were difficult to design and were fragile.

Improved Success

Current improved interventions however, include smoke hoods which operate in much the same manner as flues, to extract smoke, but are found to reduce levels of IAP more effectively than homes that relied solely on windows for ventilation. Some features of newly improved stoves include a chimney, enclosing the fire to retain heat, designing a pot holder to maximize heat transfer, dampers to control air flow, a ceramic insert to reduce heat loss, and multi-pot systems to allow for cooking multiple dishes.

Stoves are now known to be one of the least-cost means to achieve the combined objective of reducing the health burden of IAP and in some areas reducing environmental stress from biomass harvesting. Some success in installation of interventions, including improved cook stoves, has been achieved primarily due to an interdisciplinary approach which includes multiple stakeholders. These projects have discovered that key socio-economic issues must be addressed to ensure the success of intervention programs. A multitude of complex issues indicate improved stoves are not merely a tool to save fuel.

Kenya Smoke and Health Project

The following information represents one successful intervention known as the Kenya Smoke and Health Project (1998-2001) which involved fifty rural households in two separate regions, Kajiado and West Kenya. These areas were chosen due to different climate, geographic, and cultural implications. Community participation was the primary focus for this project and as a result, those involved indicated the results far exceeded their expectations. Local women's groups and, in the case of the project in West Kenya, men were actively involved. By involving the end-users the project resulted in more widespread acceptance and created the further benefit of providing local income.

Three key interventions were discussed and disseminated; ventilation by enlarging windows or opening eaves spaces, adding smoke hoods over the cooking area, or the option of installing an improved cook stove such as the Upesi stove. Smoke hoods are free-standing units that act like flues or chimneys in their effort to draw smoke out of the dwelling. They can be used over traditional open fires and this study showed they contribute to considerably lower levels of IAP. The smoke hood models were made with hard manila paper and then transferred to heavy-gauge galvanized sheet metal and manufactured locally. This resulted in further employment opportunities for the artisans who were trained by the project. The Upesi stove, made of clay and kiln-fired, was developed by Practical Action and East African partners to utilize wood and agricultural wastes. Because this stove was designed and adapted for local needs it produced several winning features. Not only does it cut the use of fuel-wood by approximately half, and reduce exposure to household smoke, it also empowers local women by creating employment as they are the ones who make and market the stoves. These women's groups gain access to technical training in production and marketing and enjoy higher wage earnings and improved social status as a result of the introduction of this improved stove.

Benefits

Various benefits were realized including improved health; the most important aspect to each of the villagers involved. The people reported less internal heat allowing for better sleep, fewer headaches and less fatigue, less eye irritation and coughs and dizziness. Safety increased due to the smoke hoods preventing goats and children from falling into the fire and less soot contamination was observed, along with snakes and rodents not entering the home. Windows allowed for the ability to view cattle from indoors, and also reduced kerosene needs due to improved interior lighting. Overall, the indoor environment improved greatly from various simple things that are taken for granted in modern western homes. Greater indoor light also allows for more income generation for women as they can do beadwork by the window when weather doesn't allow for this work outdoors. Children also benefit from increased lighting for homework.

Interpersonal relationships developed among the women due to the project, and men better supported their wives initiative when the end result benefited them as well. While initial efforts to improve stoves were limited in success, current efforts are more successful due to the recognition that sustainable domestic energy resources are "central to reducing poverty and hunger, improving health...and improving the lives of women and children" The optimal short-term goal in minimizing rural poverty is to provide inexpensive and acceptable solutions to the local people. Not only can stoves contribute to this intervention, but the use of cleaner fuels will also provide further benefits.

Environmental Impacts

Mortality and burden of disease are not the only detrimental effects from utilizing inefficient energy technology such as the combustion of biomass. Kenya's pre-dominant energy source is biomass, providing more than 90 per cent of rural household energy needs, about one-third in the form of charcoal and the rest from firewood. Biomass energy sourced primarily from savannah woodlands includes firewood for inhabitants and charcoal for urban use. A small percentage is sourced by neighboring communities from closed and protected forests which are generally found in high population density areas. While biomass harvesting in sensitive areas is problematic, it is now determined that the great majority of biomass clearing is due to agricultural expansion and land conversion. Approximately 38% of households 'in high agro-ecological zones' utilize agricultural waste due to frequent shortages of conventional fuel-wood. Use of crop residue and animal waste for domestic energy has detrimental results on soil quality and agricultural and livestock productivity. These materials are ultimately not available as soil conditioners, organic fertilizer, and livestock fodder, not to mention the "cumulative effects on national food security".

Most farmers are aware however, that when agricultural waste and dung are not used for energy, they are important elements to maintaining soil fertility. One of the most efficient ways to utilize crop waste and dung for domestic energy is to produce briquettes. The process of compacting the material into a donut shape creates more efficient combustion which contributes to reduced emission levels. A simple device allows for this process and it can be done locally.

Sustainable Options

Large-scale combustion of biomass is only feasible if carried out in a sustainable manner. Concern is paramount for regeneration of renewable and sustainable fuel-wood sources if it is to continue to be available long-term. Attempts at sustainable solutions in Kenya could include developing energy crops (trees and shrubs) which would also provide additional income for farmers. This solution would benefit cropland or rangeland prone to erosion and flooding as the root systems and leaf litter would enhance soil stability. Careful selection of regenerating varieties would be most sustainable because soil stability is not disrupted due to tilling and planting. Some people view this solution as a way to further exploit forests, but with proper management of forest resources this could be a viable solution.

Challenges

Widespread education and government funding will also be necessary to shift cultural practices to more sustainable energy use. For example, in an area in South Africa, even though access to electricity was available, many residents continued to use biomass fuels for cooking and heating due to cost of electrical appliances and cultural practices. Liquid petroleum gas (LPG), which has nearly 100% combustion and negligible emissions unfortunately is currently not cost effective. The use of solar power, such as solar cookers, has drawbacks in practical use because they must be used outdoors, and they are slow and do not work in the evening or on cloudy days.

Education Interventions

Educational intervention can contribute to reducing exposure to smoke by developing a social marketing effort in alerting people to the dangers and encouraging a willingness to alter living and cultural practices which could have a significant impact on mitigating exposure to IAP. These interventions "must be based on felt needs..." with emphasis and sensitivity to gender issues. Evidence of one successful government intervention was revealed by China who, between 1980 and 1995, disseminated 172 million improved cookstoves. This effort proved more successful due to the inclusion of local users, particularly women, who were involved in the design and fieldwork process.

Kenya and Modern Energy

As of 2004, Kenya has shown a willingness to undertake biomass energy issues with the understanding that consumption is associated with indoor air pollution and environmental degradation. Suggestions from the United Nations Development Programme include establishing an institution that will deal exclusively with biomass energy by developing policy guidelines on sustainable firewood, charcoal, and modern biomass such as cleaner fuels and wind, solar, and small scale hydropower. Short-term solutions rest in more efficient domestic energy use by way of improved cook stoves which provide more affordable options in the near future than a complete shift to nonsolid fuels. Long-term solutions rest on transition to modern cleaner fuels and alternative energy sources within a broad international and national policy and economic agenda. Government support for long-term solutions is feasible as witnessed by current efforts in Zambia to develop policy to promote biofuels.

Further Action

National and international effort must be stepped up to advance short and long term solutions for the millions of women and children who suffer from poverty and disease as a result of indoor air pollution. Scientists predict the African continent will be the first to experience the effects of global warming where widespread poverty will put millions at further risk due to their limited capabilities to adapt. The potential is great for a more sustainable Africa with commitment from within and outside the region.

REFERENCES

Salthammer, T.(ed.) 1999. "Organic Indoor Air Pollutants — Occurrence, Measurement, Evaluation". Wiley-VCH, Germany.

Spengler, J.D. and Samet, J.M. (1991). "Indoor Air Pollution: A Health Perspective". Johns Hopkins University Press, Baltimore.

Spengler, J.D., Samet, J.M. & McCarthy, J.F (2001). "Indoor Air Quality Handbook". McGraw–Hill, NY. ISBN 0-07-445549-4.

http://www.epa.gov/ebtpages/airindoorairpollution.html - Website of the United States Environmental Protection Agency (US EPA)

^ [1] DOE EERE Indoor Air Quality - MERV 13 Air Filters

BuildingEcology.com. http://www.buildingecology.com. Links to a Large Number of Resources for Information on Indoor Air Quality.

The Air Act

THE AIR (PREVENTION AND CONTROL OF POLLUTION) ACT, 1981

DEPARTMENT OF ENVIRONMENT

NOTIFICATION

New Delhi, the 18 November, 1982

G.S.R. 712(E): In exercise of the powers conferred by section 53 of Air Prevention and Control of Pollution) Act, 1981 (14 of 1981) the Central Government in consultation with the Central Board for the Prevention and Control of Water Pollution hereby makes the following rules, namely:

CHAPTER 1

PRELIMINARY

1. Short title and commencement

(1) These rules may be called the Air (Prevention and Control of Pollution) Rules, 1982.

(2) They shall come into force on the date of their publication in the Official Gazette.

2. Definitions

In these rules unless the context otherwise requires.

(a) "Act" means the Air (Prevention and Control of Pollution) Act, 1981;

(b) "Chairman" means the Chairman of the Central Board;

(c) "form" means a form set out in the Schedules;

(d) "meeting" means a meeting of the Central Board or a meeting of Committee constituted by the Central Board;

(e) "member Secretary" means the member secretary of the Central Board;

(f) "Schedule" means a Schedule appended to these rules;

(g) "section" means a section of the Act;

(h) "year" means the financial year commencing on the 1st day of April;

(i) words and expressions not defined in these rules but defined in the Act shall have the meaning assigned to them in the Act.

CHAPTER 2

PROCEDURE FOR TRANSACTION OF BUSINESS OF THE BOARD AND ITS COMMITTEES

3. Notice of meetings

(1) Meeting of the Central Board shall be held on such dates as may be fixed by the Chairman.

(2) The Chairman shall, upon a written request of not less than five members of the Central Board or upon a direction of the Central Government, call a special meeting of the Central Board.

(3) Fifteen clear days' notice of an ordinary meeting and three days' notice of a special meeting specifying the time and the place at which such meeting is to be held and an agenda of business to be transacted thereat, shall be given by the member-secretary or Chairman to the members or any other officers of the Board.

(4) Notice of the meeting may be given to the members by delivering the same by messenger or sending it

by registered post to his last known place of S residence or business or in such other manner as- the Chairman may, in the circumstances of the case, think fit.

(5) No member shall be entitled to bring forward for the consideration of a meeting any matter of which he has not given ten clear-day's notice to the member Secretary unless the Chairman, in his discretion, permits him to do so.

(6) If the Chairman or presiding officer adjourns a meeting from day to day or any particular day he shall give reason thereof and no fresh notice shall be required for such an adjourned meeting.

4. Presiding Officer

Every meeting shall be presided over by the Chairman and in his absence, by a presiding officer to be of elected by the members present from amongst themselves.

5. All questions to be decided by majority.

(1) All questions at a meeting shall be decided by-a majority of votes of members present and voting shall be by raising of hands in favour of the proposal.

(2) In case of an equality of votes, the Chairman or presiding officer shall have a second or casting vote.

6. Quorum

(1) Five members shall form the quorum for any meeting.

(2) If at any time fixed for any meeting or during the course of any meeting a quorum is not present, the Chairman or presiding member shall adjoin the meeting and if a quorum is not present after the expiration of fifteen minutes from such adjournment, the presiding officer shall adjourn the meeting to such time on the following or on such other future date as he may fix.

(3) If the meeting is adjourned to some future date due to lack of quorum, fresh notice will be given to the absentee members as to the date and time on which the next meeting will be held.

(4) No matter which had not been on the agenda of the original meeting shall be discussed at such adjourned meeting.

7. Minutes

(1) Record of the proceedings of every meeting along with the names of members who attended the meeting shall be kept by the member-secretary in a book maintained by him exclusively for the purpose.

(2) The minutes of the previous meeting shall be read at the beginning of every succeeding meeting and shall be confirmed and signed by the Chairman or presiding officer at such meeting.

(3) The proceedings shall be open to inspection by any member at the once of the Central Board during office hours.

8. Maintaining order at meetings

The Chairman or presiding officer shall preserve order at a meeting.

9. Business to be transacted at a meeting

(1) No business shall be transacted in the meeting without quorum.

(2) Except with the permission of the chairman or presiding officer, no business which is not entered in the agenda or of which notice has not been given by a member under sub-rule (5) of the rule 3, shall be transacted at any meeting.

10. Order of business

(1) At any meeting business shall be transacted in the order in which it is entered in the agenda circulated to the members under sub-rule (3) of rule 3.

(2) Either at the beginning of the meeting or after the conclusion of the debate on a motion during the meting, the Chairman or presiding officer or a member may suggest a change in the order of business as entered in the agenda and if the majority of the members present agree, the Chairman or presiding officer shall agree to such a change.

11. Procedure for transaction of business of committees constituted by the Board under sub-section (1) of Section 11

(1) The time and place of the meting of a committee constituted by the Central Board under sub-section (I) of section 11 shall be as specified by the Chairman of the committee.

(2) Provision of Chapter-2 of these rules shall as far as practicable, apply to the meeting of the committee constituted under section 11.

CHAPTER 3

12. A member of a committee other than a member of the Board shall be paid an allowance of rupees fifty if he is a resident of Delhi and rupees seventy-five (inclusive of daily allowance 3 and also travelling allowance at such rate as is admissible to a grade I officer of the Central Government in the case of non resident, for each day of the actual meeting of the committee which he attends.

Provided that in case of a member of Parliament who is also a member of the Central Board, the said daily and travelling allowances will be admissible when the Parliament is not in session and on production of a certificate by the member that he has not drawn any such allowance for the same journey and halts from any other Government source.

CHAPTER 4

TEMPORARY ASSOCIATION OF PERSONS WITH THE CENTRAL BOARD

13. Manner and purpose of Association of persons with the Central Board under sub-section (1) of section 12.

The Central Board may invite any person whose assistance or advise is considered useful in performing any of its functions, to participate in the deliberations of any of its meetings or the meetings of a committee formed by it.

14. Fees and allowances to be paid to such temporary association of persons under sub-section (3) of section 12.

(1) If the person associated with the Board under rule 13 happens to be a non-official resident in Delhi, he shall be entitled to get an allowance of rupees fifty per day for each day of actual meeting of the Central Board in which he is so associated.

(2) If such person is non-resident of Delhi, he shall be entitled to get an allowance of rupees seventy five per day (inclusive of daily allowance) for each day of actual meeting of the Central Board when he is so associated and also to travelling allowance at such rates as is admissible to a grade I officer of the Central Government.

(3) Notwithstanding anything in sub-rules (I) and (2) if such person is a

Government servant or an employee in a Government undertaking, he shall be entitled to travelling and daily allowances only at the rates admissible under the relevant rules applicable to him:

Provided that in case of a member of Parliament who is also a member of the Central Board, the said daily and travelling allowances will be admissible when the Parliament is not in session and on production of a certificate by the member that he has not drawn any such allowance for the same journey and halts from any other Government source.

CHAPTER 5

BUDGET OFTHE CENTRAL BOARD

15. Form of budget estimates under section 34.

(1) The form in which and time within which the budget may be prepared and provided and forwarded to the government shall be as provided in forms I, II, III and IV of Schedule 1.

(2) The estimated receipts and expenditure shall be accompanied by the revised budget estimates for the current year.

(3) The budget shall, as far as may be, based on the account heads specified in Schedule 11.

CHAPTER 6

ANNUAL REPORT OFTHE CENTRAL BOARD

16. Form of Annual Report under section 35.

The annual report in respect of the year last ended giving a true and full account of the activities of the Central Board during the previous financial year shall contain the particulars specified in Schedule 111 and shall be submitted to the Central Government by 15th of May each year.

CHAPTER 7

ACCOUNT OF THE CENTRALBOARD

17. Form of annual statement of accounts of the Central Board under section 36.

The annual statement of accounts of the Central Board shall be in forms V to IX.

[Q. 16013/2/81-FPC]
N.D. JAYAL, Joint Secretary
Department of Environment

SCHEDULE I

FORM I

CENTRAL POLLUTION CONTROL BOARD

Detailed Budget Estimates for the Year 19

(See rule 15)

ADMINISTRATION

(Expenditure)

Heads of Accounts	Actuals of the past three years			Sanctioned estimate for the current year 19.....	Actuals of last six months i.e., 19.... 19....	Actuals of six months current year 19.....	Revised estimate for the current year 19.....	Budget Estimate for the next year 19....	Variations between columns 5 & 8	Variations between columns 8 & 9	Explanation for columns 10 &11
	19	19	19								
1	2	3	4	5	6	7	8	9	10	11	12

FORM II
CENTRAL POLLUTION CONTROL BOARD
ESTABLISHMENT

Statement details of provision for pay of officers/Establishment for the year 19...-19....
(See rule 15)

1	2	3			4	5			6	7
Name and designation	Reference to page of estimate form	Sanctioned pay of the Post			Amount of provisions for the year at the rate in column	Increment falling due within the year			Total provision for the year i.e. total columns 4 & 5	Remarks
		Minimum/Maximum Actual pay of the person concerned due on 1st April next year				Date of increment	Rate of increment	Amount of increment for the year		
		(a)	(b)	(c)	3(c)	(a)	(b)	(c)		

FORM III
CENTRAL POLLUTION CONTROL BOARD
NOMINAL ROLLS
(See rule 15)

Name and designation	Pay	Dearness allowance	City compensatory allowance	House rent allowance	Over-time allowance	Children educational allowance	Leave travel concession	Other allowances	Total
1	2	3	4	5	6	7	8	9	10
Total									

FORM IV

CENTRAL POLLUTION CONTROL BOARD

(Abstract of Nominal Rolls)

(See rule 15)

Actual sanctioned strength as on 1st March, 19...	Particulars of posts	Sanctioned budget grant 19... - 19...		Revised Estimates 19... - 19...		Budget estimates 19... - 19...		Explanation for the difference between sanctioned budget grant revised estimates and budget estimates.
		No. of posts included	Pay and allowances	No. of posts included	Pay and allowances	No. of posts included	Pay and allowances	
1	2	3	4	5	6	7	8	9
	I. Officers							
	(a) Posts filled							
	(b) Posts vacant							
	Total I Officers							
	II. Establishment							
	(a) Posts filled							
	(b) Posts vacant							
	Total II Establishment							
	III. Class IX							
	(a) Posts filled							
	(b) Posts vacant							
	Total III-Class IV							
	Grand Total - I, II and III							

SCHEDULE II

BUDGET AND ACCOUNT HEADS [See rule 15(3)]

ADMINISTRATION

Heads of Accounts (Expenditure)

1. Salaries.
2. Wages.
3. Travel expenses.
4. Office expenses.
   (a) Furniture.
   (b) Postage.
   (c) Office machines/equipment
   (d) Liveries.
   (e) Hot and cold weather charges.
   (f) Telephones.
   (g) Electricity and water charges
   (h) Stationery.
   (i) Printing.
   (j) Staff car and other vehicles.
   (k) Other items.
5. Fee and honoraria.
6. Payment for professional and special services.
7. Rents, rates and taxes/royalty.
8. Publications.
9. Advertising sales and publicity expenses.
10. Grants in aid/contributions/subsidies.
11. Hospitality expenses sumptuary allowances etc.
12. Pensions/gratuities.
13. Write off/losses.
14. Suspenses.
15. Expenses in connection with the setting up and maintenance of the Board laboratory.
16. Other charges (a residuary head, this will al ,o include rewards and prizes).

Heads of Account (Receipts).

1. Payments by Central Government.
2. Fees.
3. Fines and other receipts.

1[SCHEDULE III]

(See Rule 16)

CENTRAL POLLUTION CONTROL BOARD
ANNUAL REPORT FOR THE FINANCIAL YEAR

APRIL 1, 19... TO MARCH 31, 19...

CHAPTER-1 : Introduction

CHAPTER-2 : Constitution of the Board including changes therein.

CHAPTER-3 : Meeting of the Board with major decisions taken therein.

CHAPTER-4 : Committees constituted by the Board and their activities.

CHAPTER-5 : Monitoring Network for air, water and soil quality.

CHAPTER-6 : Present state of environment environmental problems and counter measures.

CHAPTER-7 : Environmental Research.

CHAPTER-8 : Environmental Training.

CHAPTER-9 : Environmental Awareness and Public Participation.

CHAPTER-10 : Environmental Standards including time schedule for their enforcement

CHAPTER-11.1 : Prosecutions launched and convictions secured for environmental pollution control.

CHAPTER-11.2 : Directions given for closure of polluting industrial units.

CHAPTER-12 : Finance and accounts of the Board.

CHAPTER-13 : Annual Plan of the following year.

CHAPTER-14 : Any other important matter dealt with by the Central Board.

ANNEXURES

1. Members of the Board.
2. Organisation Chart.
3. Staff Strength including recruitment.
4. Publications.
5. Training Courses/Seminars/Workshops organised or attended.
6. Consents to establish industries, operations & processes-issued/ refused.
7. Consents to operate industries operations & process-issued/refused

[F.No. Z-20013/4/91-CPW]
MUKUL SANWAL, Jt. Secy.

FORM V

CENTRAL POLLUTION CONTROL BOARD

Receipts and payments for the year ended

(See rule 17)

Previous year	Receipts	Previous year	Payments
1	2	3	4
Opening Balance ______ I. Grants received ______ (a) from Government ______ (b) from other agencies ______ II. Fees ______ III. Fines and Forfeitures. IV. Interest of investments. V. Miscellaneous Receipts. VI. Miscellaneous Advances. VII. Deposits TOTAL ______		1. Capital Expenditure (i) Works (ii) Fixed Assets (iii) Other Assets (a) Laboratory Equipment (b) Vehicles (c) Furnitures and Fixtures (d) Scientific Instruments and office appliances (e) Tools and Plant 2. Revenue Expenditure (A) Administrative (i) Pay of Officers (ii) Pay of Establishment (iii) Allowances and Honoraria (iv) Leave Salary and Pension Contributions (v) Contingent Expenditure Deduct Recoveries	

(Contd...)

<table>
<tr><td colspan="1"></td><td colspan="2">(B)
(i) Board Laboratory.
(ii) Charges to be paid to the Central Water Laboratory.
(C) Running and Maintenance of vehicles
(D) Maintenance and Repairs
(i) Building and land Drainage including rents, if any
(ii) Works
(iii) Furniture and Fixtures
(iv) Scientific Instruments and Office Appliances
(v) Tools and Plants
(vi) Temporary works (including maintenance and repairs)
(E) Fees to Consultants and Specialists
(F) Law charges
(G) Miscellaneous
(H) Fees for Audit
3. Purchases ____________
4. Miscellaneous ____________
5. Advances ____________
6. Deposits ____________
Closing Balance ____________
Total ____________</td></tr>
<tr><td>Accounts Officer</td><td>Member Secretary</td><td>Chairman</td></tr>
</table>

Expenditure					Income		
Previous year	Details	Total of sub-head	Total of major head	Previous year	Details	Total of sub-head	Total of major head
1	2	3	4	5	6	7	8
To					By		
REVENUE EXPENDITURE					(I) GRANTS RECEIVED		
(A) Administrative:					(a) From Government		
(i) Pay of Officers					(b) From other agencies.		
(ii) Pay of establishment					Total:		
(iii) Allowances & Honoraria					Less:		
(iv) Leave salary and Pension Contributions					Amount utilised for capital expenditure net grant available for Revenue expenditure		
(v) Board's Contributions to the staff Provident Fund					(II) Fees		
(vi) Contigent expenditure Deduct Recoveries					(III) Service Rental Charges.		
(B) Running Expenses of Laboratories:					(IV) Fines and Forfeitures.		
(i) Main Laboratory					(V) Interest on investments.		
(ii) Payments to be made to Central Water Laboratory					(VI) Miscellaneous Receipts.		
(C) Running Water and Maintenance of Vehicles					(VII) Excess of expenditure over incoem.		
(D) Maintenance and Repairs:					Total:		
(i) Building and Land Drainage							
(ii) Works							
(iii) Furnitures & Fixtures							
(iv) Scientific instruments and office appliances.							
(v) Tools and Plants							

FORM VI

CENTRAL POLLUTION CONTROL BOARD

ANNUAL STATEMENT OF ACCOUNTS

Income and Expenditure Account for the year ended 31st March, 19__

(See rule 17)

FORM VII

CENTRAL POLLUTION CONTROL BOARD

ANNUAL STATEMENT OF ACCOUNTS

Balance Sheet as at 31st March, 19....

(See rule 17)

Capital and Liabilities				Property and Assets			
Previous year	Details	Total of sub-head	Total of major head	Previous year	Details	Total of sub-head	Total of major head
1	2	3	4	5	6	7	8
A. Capital Fund (i) Grants received from Govt. for Capital expenditure. (a) Amount utilised upto 31st March 19__ (b) Unutilised balance on 31st March 19__ (ii) Grant from other agencies for Capital expenditure (a) Amount utilised upto 31st March 19__ (b) Unutilised balance on 31st March 19__ (iii) Value of land provided by Govt. (per contra)				1. Works- (As per Form VIII) 2. Fixed Assets (As per Form IX) (a) Value of land provided by Govt. (at cost). (b) Buildings- Balance as per last Balance sheet			

(Contd...)

1	2	3	4	5	6	7	8
B. Capital Receipts C. (i) Deposits received for works from Outside bodies- (ii) Deposits- Less Expenditure- (iii) Other deposits- D. Amounts due- (i) Purchases (ii) Others- E. Excess of income over expenditure- (i) upto 31st March 19.. . (ii) Add for the year (iii) Deduct-Excess of Expenditure over income				Additions during the year Total Less: Depreciation during the year Total: 3. Other Assets (As per Form IX) (a) Laboratory equipment as per last balance sheet additions during the year Total: Less: Depreciation during the year Total: (b) Vehicles as per last balance sheet. Additions during the year. Total: Less: Depreciation during the year Total: (c) Furniture and Fixtures. As per last Balance Sheet. Additions during the year. Total:			

(Contd...)

1	2	3	4	5	6	7	8
				(d) Scientific Instruments and Office. Appliances- As per last Balance Sheet. Additions during the year Total: (e) Tools and Plants As per last Balance Sheet Additions during the year Total: Less: Depreciation during the year.			
4. Sundry Debtors-				Total: (i) Amounts due from outside bodies for expenditure incurred- Expenditure Less amount received (ii) Other Sundry Debtors 5. Advances (a) Miscellaneous Advances. (b) Cash at Bank (c) Cash in hand (d) Cash in transit			
Total-				Total			
Accounts Officer				Member-Secretary			Chairman

FORM VIII
CENTRAL POLLUTION CONTROL BOARD)
ANNUAL STATEMENT OF ACCOUNT
Expenditure on works as on 3Ist March, 19
(Item I-Asset of the Balance Sheet)
(See Rule 17)

Sl. No.	Name of work	Upto 3lst March 19			During the year 19			Upto 31st March 19		
		Direct Expenditure	Overhead Charges	Total Expenditure	Direct Expenditure	Overhead Charges	Total Expenditure	Direct Expenditure	Overhead Charges	Total Expenditure
TOTAL										
Accounts Officer			Member-Secretary			Chairman				

FORM IX

CENTRAL POLLUTION CONTROL BOARD

ANNUAL STATEMENT OF ACCOUNTS

Fixed Assets as on 31st March, 19 (Item 2 Assets to the Balance Sheet).

Other Assets as on 31st March, 19 (Item 3 Assets to the Balance Sheet).

(See Rule 17)

Sl. No.	Particulars of Assets	Balance as on 31st March 19	Additions during the years	Total	Depreciation during the year	Sales of write off during the year	Balance as on 31st March 19	Cumulative Depreciation as on 31st March 19
Accounts Officer				Member-Secretary				Chairman

Air Pollution Meteorology

Meteorology (from Greek: μετέωρο, meteron, "high in the sky"; and λόγος, logos, "knowledge") is the interdisciplinary scientific study of the atmosphere that focuses on weather processes and forecasting. Meteorological phenomena are observable weather events which illuminate and are explained by the science of meteorology. Those events are bound by the variables that exist in Earth's atmosphere. They are temperature, pressure, water vapor, and the gradients and interactions of each variable, and how they change in time. The majority of Earth's observed weather is located in the troposphere.

Meteorology, climatology, atmospheric physics, and atmospheric chemistry are sub-disciplines of the atmospheric sciences. Meteorology and hydrology comprise the interdisciplinary field of hydrometeorology.

Interactions between our atmosphere and the oceans are part of coupled ocean-atmosphere studies. Meteorology has application in many diverse fields such as the military, energy production, farming, shipping and construction.

Factor Affecting Air Pollution

Number of factor affecting the dispersion and concentration of air pollutants in the ambient environment, these are:

1. **Wind:** wind change the temperature of one place according to the areas from which they flow. The prevailing winds, in temperature latitutdes, coming from the land area lower the temperature. In winter and raise it in summer. In contrast the prevailing winds coming from the sea areas raise the winter temperature, but lower the summer temperature.

   Thus direction from which the wind blows determines wheather that wind will be cool or warm. If the wind blows from a warm place, the wind will be warm and if it blows from a cool place it will be cool.

   Winds also bring rain with them, when winds blow over seas and ocean and other bodies of water they carry some of the water vapour blows across the land, it cools and water vapour turns into clouds and fall to the earth as rain. If the temperature of the rain is low, the water vapous may turn to snow.

   Winds can take pollutants go one place to another place. It has been noticed that dust particle of south Arabia come in India by wind. Winds also responsible for the dispersion of pollutants. These dispersion is vertical as well as horizontal movermebnt.

2. **Wind roses:** it indicates the direction form which the wind comes. It follows that pollution is carried to the opposite quadrant i.e., a south west wind depostes the pollutants carries to north-east.

3. **Separated flows:** the separation of flows around building can cause high concentration of pollutants in the down stream separated region. The separation behind a stack will also result in down wash of the effluent trapped in the separated region. Thus the plume may not rise above the stack level and may even be carried downward on the back side of stack. This happens when the stack velocity is about equal to on less then the ambient velocity.

   If Vs < Va (Vs = Velocity of stack. Va velocity of air), then pollutants can not be disperse in air, it is called down stream.

4. **Turbulent flow diffusion:** The change in velocity with height is a function both of terrain and of the time of day. Air flow can be modeled as turbulent flow with the turbulence represented by eddy motion. An eddy means a piece of air which moves randomly in a fluctuating manner. During the day, the heat cause thermal turbulence, so turbulent mixing is increased and wind profile is flatter than at night. The second type of turbulence mechanical turbulence is cause by earth or man made.

   It has been discovered that small eddi

Plume Behavior

Plume refers to the path and extent of the gaseous effluents, released from a stack, in the atmosphere. The behavior of plume released form a stack depends on localized atmosphere stability. Typical situations generally encountered in the lower atmosphere (< 300 m above ground level). Plume behavior can be following six types:

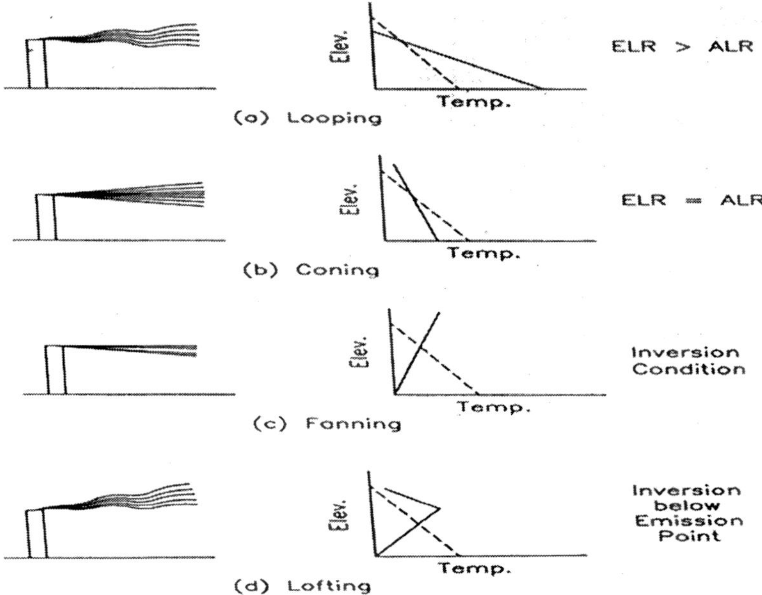

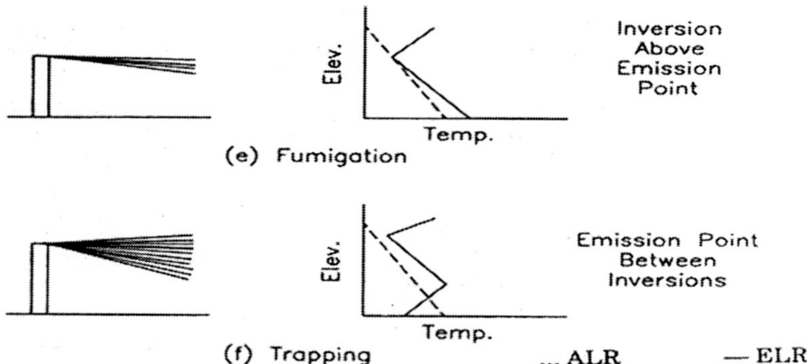

(e) Fumigation

(f) Trapping

(i) **Looping:** This type of plume has a way shape, and it occurs in a highly unstable atmosphere when rapid mixing takes place. The high degree of turbulence helps in dispersing the plume rapidly, but high concentrations may occur near the stack if the plume touches the ground.

(ii) **Coning:** It is a cone shaped, with horizontal axis, plume. It occurs in near neutral (stable) atmosphere when wind velocity is greater than 32 km/hr (i.e. windy conditions). However, the plume reaches the ground at a greater distance than looping plume. Also concentration is less, but it persists longer than the looping plume.

(iii) **Fanning:** This type of plume is emitted under extreme inversion conditions. Under these conditions, the plume spreads horizontally (fan shaped) and there is very little vertical spreading for kilometers down – wind. It dispersed very slowly.

(iv) **Lofting:** This type of plume is in the form of loops or cones with well-defined bottom. Lofting occurs when there is a strong lapse rate above a surface inversion. Under such conditions, diffusion is rapid upward, but downward diffusion does not penetrate the inversion layer. Under these conditions, emission will not reach the ground surface. It is considered to the best condition for dispersion because the pollutants are dispersed in the upper air with very little probability of ground contact.

(v) **Fumigation:** It is a phenomenon, when pollutants (that are aloft in the air) are brought rapidly to ground level when the air destabilizes. The plume is in the form of a well-defined cone with dragged or diffused bottom. Under these conditions, the concentration is relatively high and the probability of ground contact is also very high.

(vi) **Trapping:** This refers to conditions, when the plume is sand-witched between inversions and, thus, can only diffuse with in a limited vertical height.

The lofting plume is the most favorable with regard to minimizing air pollution. While, the fumigating and trapping plumes are very critical for ground level pollution concentrations point of view. Observation of smoke plumes is useful in determining the location at which the air samples should be taken. The knowledge of characteristics of plume is also helpful in dealing with the invisible pollutants.

Environmental Management

The pattern of development which we have been following and the greed of the modern society to achieve every thing which nature has as a resource, have resulted in massive degeneration of our environment, depletion of natural resources and pollution of our environment, which is posing a threat to destroy the vital life support system of our planet earth. Entire humanity has not prospered by the exploitation of natural resources, two third of world's population still lives in shabby hutments, in wants, in misery and very poor unhygienic conditions.

To improve the lot of world's poor under-developed citizens, on one hand we have to accelerate economic development which will built up our capacity to protect the environment and, on the other hand this development should be conservation linked development or say it should be a sustainable development, i.e. a development which provides for the legitimate needs of present generation without comprising the ability of future generations to meet their own needs.

When we say environmental management we mean that to manage different types of problems which exist because of the deterioration of the conditions which are needed for the better living of human society and sustaining the natural processes.

Our objectives of environmental management should thus include following:

1. To provide for the legitimate needs of all people of the present generation and to bring them to a reasonable standards of life.
2. To manage economic development in such a way as to enhance and widen our resource base so that the ability of our future generation, which is likely to be more numerous than we are, to meet their own needs is not compromised.
3. To protect and preserve the environmental quality for the present and future generations.

Environmental Management Strategies

It has been the cumulative action, spread over several decades of so many people all over the world which has caused the degeneration of our natural resources and adverse changes in the environment of today.

- Though a large share of responsibility of bringing these changes goes to the industrialized countries of the world, but each locality, each region and each country has contributed to it in one way or other.
- Local or regional problems concerning environment as well as global issues which confront humanity to day have to be simultaneously addressed as it is many of the local problems only which add up to assume global dimensions.
- Emission of different gases from a small industrial unit, smoke coming out from a tiny power plant, automobile exhaust etc. while cause a local nuisance, but also add a little bit to the global burden of green house gases.
- Similarly, CFCs used and released from each small or large township while apparently causing no local problems could contribute a little to the ozone depleting substances of the stratosphere.
- Diverse means and methods are being used by environmentally conscious people all over the world to

redress the environmental problems. But in general most of the efforts being carried out to protect the natural resources, wildlife, environment and building up a sustainable society and these include:

- Environmental Education
- Sustainable use of natural resources
- Checking environmental pollution and stabilizing global chemical cycles
- Halting degeneration of biodiversity
- Placing a check on population growth.

1. Environmental Education

- Environmental education has a fundamental role to play in motivating people to adopt environmental friendly practices.
- We cannot expect people to act in appropriate way without an awareness of the problems. It causes, the impact on our daily life and the long range consequences.
- Many problems concerning environment and biosphere are simply there because so many people contribute little bits and pieces to it, all of which put together assume enormous dimensions.
- A little efforts, a little care exercised by each individual in the society could eliminate the entire problem. Starting from grass-root levels environmental education should involve all section of our society and should be able to:
  (i) Create a general awareness concerning environmental problems
  (ii) Motivate people to conserve resources, protect environment and avoid extravagence.
  (iii) Promote understanding and co-operation among people to face ecological issues.
  (iv) Conserve indigenous knowledge, tradition and culture friendly to the environment.

(i) Creating a general awareness concerning environmental problems

A number of ecologically damaging activities could be stopped simply by providing adequate understanding of the consequences by involving to the people who indulge in such activities. Individuals, communities and human so as a whole should acquire the skill, will and experience to act singly as well as collectively to face the problem of environment.

(ii) Motivating people to conserve resources, protect environment and avoid extravagance:

The need of the time is to preserve the normal functioning of the man dominated natural ecosystem in a healthy state. Like all other natural ecosystems, it should become self sustaining, i.e., requiring none or nominal energy and material inputs while man should satisfy himself with whatever out put it generates without over straining itself. Whenever, there is an excess output it should be shared judiciously among the needy. It is the need of the time.

(iii) Promote understanding and co-operation among people to face ecological issues

Issue related to the environmental degradation are and shall continue to be ignored in favour of economic considerations as long as gross injustices in the pattern of distribution of natural resources prevail. The establishment of new economic order both at national and at international levels, which provides for the deprived and the needy, is necessary if we are to expect something concrete from the millions of inhabitants of tropical and subtropical countries of the world. There should be a free transfer of technology and means between the developed and developing countries of the world.

(iv) Conserving indigenous knowledge, tradition and culture friendly to the environment:

Ancient traditions protect a number of plants and animal species and honour sacred grooves believed to be the homes of God.Much of this accumulated wisdom of past is to be saved.

2. Sustainable use of natural resources

Natural resources such as mineral wealth, fossil fuels, fertile soils, fresh water, live-stock and fisheries, wild life and forests etc. provide the mankind with everything which is needed directly or indirectly. These resources can be renewable or non-renewable. Renewable resources are those resources which can be regenerated whereas non-renewable resources are those resources which can not be regenerated once they are exhausted. Both the renewable resources and non-renewable resources have their own limitations.

Since a constant flow of materials is needed to maintain the loving beings, the society and economy, it is not one way consumption but a regular re-use and recycling which has so far enabled the biosphere to maintain it self since life began on this planet. Sustainable management of natural resources, therefore, involves different type of strategies for renewable and non renewable resources.

(a) Sustainable management of non-renewable resources

The sustainable management of our mineral wealth involves strategies to extend their life span which may be carried out by following:

1. Economy in the use of mineral resources, reduction in wastage and whenever possible the use of some cheaper substitute.
2. Re-use and recycling which shall reduce the demand on virgin material.
3. Making finished products that are long lasting which shall have the effect of decreasing the demand of the commodity, reducing thereby the demand of the metal concerned.
4. More efficient recovery of element from the deposits which shall curtail wastage and where smaller amounts of other elements are present in the deposits may also be tapped.
5. Protection of existing deposits and search for new ones.

(b) Sustainable management of renewable resources

Sustainable management of our renewable resources involves:

- Avoiding over-exploitation and pollution of biotic systems: There is a limit up to which natural systems can provide resources to mankind. Withdraw beyond this limit tends to damage the productivity of the system.

Both the affluence of developed countries as well as abstract poverty in under-developed countries is detrimental to the productivity of biotic systems. The root cause of environmental damage lies in want and misery of masses which inhabit developing countries of the world.

- Strengthening the resource base and augmenting regenerability of biotic systems:

  The three important sectors which feed mankind are:

  (i) Agricultural sector

  (ii) Live-stock and Fisheries

  (iii) Forest and wild life

(i) **Agricultural Sector:** Agro-ecosystems which man sets up have to be provided fresh-water nutrients or fertilizers, chemicals to suppress insects and pests ad suitable hybrid varieties. The heavy reliance of modern agriculture on material energy inputs makes it unsuitable.

The best strategy for sustainable management of agro-ecosystems appears to be the promotion of a healthy microbial community which augments nutrient regeneration capacity, water holding potential and porosity of soils.

(ii) **Live-stock and fisheries:** These provide to the mankind rich high quality proteins. For sustainable management of our livestock population we should adopt our traditional ways which served as means to convert useless organic matter left after the removal of grains from crop into a source of useful material and energy. The livestock raised on waste organic matter also serve the man to produce milk, meat, eggs, hide, woolens, manures and is a source of cheap labor. The livestock and poultry should be maintained as a useful nutrient loop between agricultural crop and man.

(iii) **Forests and wild life:** Forests and wildlife provides a variety of useful products to the mankind. For thousands of people living in world's developing countries, resources of local forests and wild life products constitute an important source of livelihood.

In addition to these, forest are helpful in checking erosion and and degradation of soils, in shaping natural environmental and local climatic conditions by maintaining humidity, regulating temperatures impeding wind velocity and influencing precipitation. With destruction of forests natural habitats for wild life are lost. The use of Agricultural food resources with a little change in our food habits and a little adjustment these species may also be used to supplement the human food. This will widen our resources base and add sustainability to supplies by reducing the dependence on a few species.

3. Checking environmental pollution and stabilizing global chemical cycles

Ever since industrialization began, about two centuries ago mankind has altered earth's chemistry drastically which may have staggering ecological and economical consequences within our life times or those of our children.

Three important out-comes of the changes in earth's chemistry brought about by industrial societies are especially threatening and costly to the entire humanity.

These are:

1. Diminishing food security from a changing climate.
2. Degeneration of forests and green cover and reduction on biodiversity.
3. Risk to humans from exposure to chemical pollutants of the environment.

The Gravity of the Problem

A large number of questions remain unanswered for each of these threats and more research is urgently needed to clear the uncertainties surrounding them.

Waiting for a definite picture to emerge could, however, be dangerous as by the time we reach any conclusion, the world will already be committed and disastrous effects inevitable and irreversible. The wise strategy would be to avoid activities detrimental to the life support system right from the very beginning.

Since 1860, we have introduced about 200 billion tons of carbon into the atmosphere. Most of this carbon was earlier trapped in fossil fuels, limestone and organic matter.

The concentration of methane, another green house gas has roughly doubled science its 1600 A.D. level.

The amount of oxide of nitrogen added to the atmosphere by human activity roughly equals the total quantity of the NO_2 produced by all natural process combined. So is the quantity of sulphur dioxide added to the atmosphere which is about 100 million tons per year.

Lead, mercury, cadmium and Zinc etc. Are some to the metals which are being deposited at many places in concentrations toxic to man and other organisms.

Management Strategies

In order to moderate the adverse impacts of human activity the following strategies are being followed:

1. Setting standards for effluents discharged in the environment.
2. Adopting more environment friendly technology.
3. Avoiding concentration of polluting industries and raising assimilative capacity of natural systems.

1. Setting standards for effluents discharged in the environment

This approach provides statuary standards for each polluting unit- be it an automobile or an industry. These standards specify permissible limits in terms of different parameters of effluent quality and the polluting unit is required to ensure that the effluent it discharge are within the specified limits.

These standards are based on evaluation of technical feasibility and economic viability. A regular monitoring of each relevant parameter is done in order to ensure that the discharges are within the prescribed limit. For example, waste water from Tannery should not have a BOD higher than 30 mg/l over 5 days period at 20° C. tanneries are required to treat their liquid effluent in such a way that BOD is reduced to levels below 30 mg/l over 5 day period at 20° C.

Thus, management based on standards distributes the responsibility of reducing the load of pollution to the polluting units.

2. Adopting more environment friendly technologies

A much better way to restrict the pollution of environmental is adoption of more environment friendly technology. For example, of the three kinds of fossil fuels in common use these days, natural gas is the least polluting sources of energy.

3. Avoiding concentration of polluting industries and raising assimilative capacity of natural systems

We can enhance this capacity of the natural system by promoting green cover in areas surroundings the industry. Barren land should be treated properly, provided fertilizers and water so that it turns into an eutrophic system - capable of supporting suitable plants and a variety of microbes so as to serve as an effective instrument of assimilation.

Placing a Check on Growth of Human Population

If we carefully mange our resources, ensure just and equitable distribution of necessities of life among all living being in this world, avoid extravagance, the planet has enough for all of us,. But the growth in population of one or two species – say for example, that of humans- cannot be indeterminate.

Howsoever, large may be the resources of a planet, whatsoever, may be its capacity for regeneration, indeterminate growth and consumption thereby, shall exhaust the carrying capacity of the system at some point of time in future and it shall collapse.

A line has to be drawn within which we shall have to confine our numbers.

Development of Concept of Environment Management System

The concept of environmental management system (EMS) emerged in early nineties, though its genesis could be traced as back as in 1972 with the beginning of UN Conference on Human Environment and launching of United Nations Environment Program. (UNEP). Later the establishment of World Commission on Environment and Development (WCED), then came Montreal Protocol and Earth Summit in 1992.

All this instigated to evolve the concept of sustainable development and environment.

The International Standard Organisation developed ISO-14001 (Standard for environment management system) in 1996.

These standards address environmental concerns through the allocation of resources, assignment of responsibilities, ongoing evaluation of practices, procedures and processes and renders practical advice on implementation of such a system.

ISO 1400 Series

These are internationally harmonized standards relating to environmental management including eco-lebelling and environmental audit etc.

- ISO 14001: EMS, Specifications with guidance
- ISO 14004: EMS, General guidelines as principles, systems and supporting techniques
- ISO 14010-12: Guide lines for environmental auditing
- ISO 14014: Initial review

- ISO 14015: Environmental Site Assessment
- ISO 14020: Environmental Labeling
- ISO 14031: Evaluation of Environmental performance
- ISO 14040-14043: Life Cycle Assessment
- ISO 14050: Terms and guidelines
- Promote voluntary consensus approach
- Sensitize internal culture in organizations
- Minimize trade barriers
- Promote predictability and consistency of national standards
- Provide frame work to move beyond compliance, reduce liabilities and employees involvement
- Enhance public posture and customer trust
- Provide credibility and performance reporting
- Installs values, changes culture and improve public image
- Provides an opportunity to link environmental objectives and targets with specific financial outcome thus ensuring that resources are made availble where they provide the most benefits in both financial and environmental terms
- Such a system reduces liabilities of accidents
- Improves relations with regulatory bodies
- Improves government-industry relations

Environment Days

February 2 World Wetland 'Day: On this day, in 1971, the Ramsar Convention on Wetlands of International Importance was signed. Wetlands are a very important part of our biodiversity and it is essential to see that they are well protected.

February 28 National Science Day: It is necessary to highlight the role of science in the protection of the environment. This day should be taken as a platform to put forward the message.

March 21 World Forestry Day: Activities such as the planting of trees and highlighting the urgency to increase the green cover.

March 22 World Water Day: The decision to celebrate this day has been taken recently as drinking water sources are fast depleting. The world must wake up to the problem and begin conserving it.

March 23 World Meteorological Day: Everyone has to be reminded that weather is an integral part of the environment.

April 7 World Health Day: The World Health Organization (WHO) was constituted on this day in 1948. In the changing environment around us health is becoming an important issue.

April 18 World Heritage Day: Environment includes not just the natural surroundings but also the manmade ones.

April 22 Earth Day: In 1970 a group of people in the United States of America got together to draw the attention of the world to the problems being caused to the earth due to modernisation. Since then this day has been celebrated all over the world as Earth Day.

May 31 Anti Tobacco Day: The world is now aware of the problems faced by not only the smokers but also the people who inhale the smoke. You can take up an anti smoking campaign in your family or the neighborhood.

June 5 World Environment Day: On this day, in 1972, the Stockholm Conference on Human Environment was held in Sweden. There was a large gathering from all over the world and people expressed their concerns for the increasing environmental problems.

July 11 World Population Day: Population has to be given special attention, as it is an ever-increasing problem especially in India.

September 16 World Ozone Day: The United Nations declared this day as the International Day for the Preservation of the Ozone Layer. It is the day the Montreal Protocol was signed.

September 28 Green Consumer Day: The problems of consumerism and its impact on the environment is an area of major concern in today's world. Awareness building on the importance of recycling-reusing-reducing should be taken up seriously.

October 3 World Habitat Day: The earth is the habitat of not only human beings but also all living creatures. Increasing human activities is threatening the habitat of other living things.

October 1-7 World Wildlife Week: Celebrate this week by building awareness on the importance of preservation of our wildlife.

October 4 World Animal Welfare Day: The welfare of animals has to be looked into and given due importance.

October 13 International Day for Natural Disaster Reduction: Due to a change in the environment there has been an increase in the number of natural disasters. Efforts have to be taken to reduce these disasters.

November 14 Children's Day in India: Children can work together for a better tomorrow by improving the environment around them.

December 2 Bhopal Tragedy Day: Mark this occasion by taking a pledge to put in your best efforts to prevent such a tragedy from occurring again.

National Air Quality Monitoring Programme (NAMP)

Central Pollution Control Board is executing a nation-wide programme of ambient air quality monitoring known as National Air Quality Monitoring Programme (NAMP). The network consist of 308 operating stations covering 115 cities/ towns in 25 States and 4 Union Territories of the country.

The objectives of the N.A.M.P. are to determine status and trends of ambient air quality; to ascertain whether the prescribed ambient air quality standards are violated. Under N.A.M.P., four air pollutants *viz.*, Sulphur Dioxide (SO_2), Oxides of Nitrogen as NO_2 and Suspended Particulate Matter (SPM) and Respirable Suspended Particulate Matter (RSPM/PM_{10}), have been identified for regular monitoring at all the locations. The monitoring of meteorological parameters such as wind speed and direction, relative humidity and temperature was also integrated with the monitoring of air quality.

The monitoring of pollutants is carried out for 24 hours (4-hourly sampling for gaseous pollutants and 8-hourly sampling for particulate matter) with a frequency of twice a week, to have 104 observations in a year. The monitoring is being carried out with the help of Central Pollution Control Board; State Pollution Control Boards: Pollution Control Committees; National Environmental Engineering Research Institute (NEERI), Nagpur. CPCB co-ordinates with these agencies to ensure the uniformity, consistency of air quality data and provides technical and financial support to them for operating the monitoring station. N.A.M.P. is being operated through various monitoring agencies, large number of personnel and equipment are involved in the sampling, chemical analyses, data reporting etc. It increases the probability of variation and personnel biases reflecting in the data, hence it is pertinent to mention that these data be treated as indicative rather than absolute.

National Ambient Air Quality Standards

Pollutants	Time-weighted average	Concentration in ambient air			Method of measurement
		Industrial areas	Residential, rural and other areas	Sensitive areas	
Sulphur Dioxide (SO_2)	Annual Average*	80 µg/m^3	60 µg/m^3	15 µg/m^3	- Improved West and Geake Method - Ultraviolet Fluorescence
	24 hours**	120 µg/m^3	80 µg/m^3	30 µg/m^3	
Oxides of Nitrogen as (NOx)	Annual Average*	80 µg/m^3	60 µg/m^3	15 µg/m^3	- Jacob & Hochheiser Modified (Na-Arsenite) Method
	24 hours**	120 µg/m^3	80 µg/m^3	30 µg/m^3	- Gas Phase Chemiluminescence
Suspended Particulate Matter (SPM)	Annual Average*	360 µg/m^3	140 µg/m^3	70 µg/m^3	- High Volume Sampling, (Average flow rate not less than 1.1 m^3/minute)
	24 hours**	500 µg/m^3	200 µg/m^3	100 µg/m^3	
Respirable Particulate Matter (RPM) (size less than 10 microns)	Annual Average*	120 µg/m^3	60 µg/m^3	50 µg/m^3	- Respirable particulate matter sampler
	24 hours**	150 µg/m^3	100 µg/m^3	75 µg/m^3	

(Contd...)

Pollutants	Time-weighted average	Concentration in ambient air			Method of measurement
		Industrial areas	Residential, Rural and other areas	Sensitive areas	
Lead (Pb)	Annual Average*	1.0 µg/m³	0.75 µg/m³	0.50 µg/m³	- ASS Method after sampling using EPM 2000 or equivalent Filter paper
	24 hours**	1.5 µg/m³	1.00 µg/m³	0.75 µg/m³	
Ammonia 1	Annual Average*	0.1 mg/ m³	0.1 mg/ m³	0.1 mg/m³	
	24 hours**	0.4 mg/m³	0.4 mg/m³	0.4 mg/m³	
Carbon Monoxide (CO)	8 hours**	5.0 mg/m³	2.0 mg/m³	1.0 mg/m³	- Non Dispersive Infra Red (NDIR)
	1 hour	10.0 mg/m³	4.0 mg/m³	2.0 mg/m³	Spectroscopy

* Annual Arithmetic mean of minimum 104 measurements in a year taken twice a week 24 hourly at uniform interval.

** 24 hourly/8 hourly values should be met 98% of the time in a year. However, 2% of the time, it may exceed but not on two consecutive days.

Global Dimming

Global dimming is the gradual reduction in the amount of global direct irradiance at the Earth's surface that was observed for several decades after the start of systematic measurements in 1950s. It is thought to have been caused by an increase in particulates such as sulfur aerosols in the atmosphere due to human action. The effect varied by location, but worldwide it was of the order of a 4% reduction over the three decades from 1960-1990. The trend reversed during the past decade. Global dimming has interfered with the hydrological cycle by reducing evaporation and may have caused droughts in some areas. Global dimming also creates a cooling effect that may have partially masked the effect of greenhouse gases on global warming.

Cause and Effects

It is thought that global dimming was probably due to the increased presence of aerosol particles in the atmosphere caused by human action. Aerosols and other particulates absorb solar energy and reflect sunlight back into space. The pollutants can also become nuclei for cloud droplets. It is also thought that the water droplets in clouds coalesce around the particles. Increased pollution causes more particulates and thereby creates clouds consisting of a greater number of smaller droplets (that is, the same amount of water is spread over more droplets). The smaller droplets make clouds more reflective, so that more incoming sunlight is reflected back into space and less reaches the earth's surface.

Clouds intercept both heat from the sun and heat radiated from the Earth. Their effects are complex and vary in time, location and altitude. Usually during the daytime the interception of sunlight predominates, giving a cooling effect; however, at night the re-radiation of heat to the Earth slows the Earth's heat loss. Also it has been thought that humans help produce the particles in the earth's atmosphere, resulting in global dimming.

Research

In the late-1960s, Mikhail Ivanovich Budyko worked with simple two-dimensional energy-balance climate models to investigate the reflectivity of ice. He found that the ice-albedo feedback created a positive feedback loop in the Earth's climate system. The more snow and ice, the more solar radiation is reflected back into space and hence the colder Earth grows and the more it snows. Other studies found that pollution or a volcano eruption could snap us into an ice age.

In the mid-1980s, Atsumu Ohmura, a geography researcher at the Swiss Federal Institute of Technology, found that solar radiation striking the Earth's surface had declined by more than 10% over the three previous decades. His findings are in apparent contradiction to global warming—the global temperature has steadily been going up. Less light reaching the earth would mean that it would have to cool. Ohmura published his findings "Secular variation of global radiation in Europe" in 1989. This was soon followed by others. Viivi Russak in 1990 "Trends of solar radiation, cloudiness and atmospheric transparency during recent decades in Estonia" and Beate Liepert in 1994 "Solar radiation in Germany - Observed trends and an assessment of their causes". Dimming has also been observed in sites all over the Former Soviet Union. Gerry Stanhill who studied these declines worldwide in many papers coined the term "Global dimming".

Independent research in Israel and the Netherlands in the late 1980s showed an apparent reduction in the amount of sunlight, despite widespread evidence that the climate was actually becoming hotter. The rate of dimming varies around the world but is on average estimated at around 2-3% per decade, with the possibility that the trend reversed in the early 1990s. It is difficult to make a precise measurement, due to the difficulty in accurately calibrating the instruments used, and the problem of spatial coverage. Nonetheless, the effect is almost certainly present.

The effect (2-3%, as above) is due to changes within the Earth's atmosphere; the value of the solar radiation at the top of the atmosphere has not changed by more than a fraction of this amount.

The effect varies greatly over the planet, but estimates of the terrestrial surface average value are:

- 5.3% (9 W/m^2); over 1958-85 (Stanhill and Moreshet, 1992)
- 2%/decade over 1964-93 (Gilgen et al, 1998)
- 2.7%/decade (total 20 W/m^2); up to 2000 (Stanhill and Cohen, 2001)
- 4% over 1961-90 (Liepert 2002)

Note that these numbers are for the terrestrial surface and not really a global average. Whether dimming (or brightening) occurred over the ocean has been a bit of an unknown though a specific measurement measured effects some 400 miles (643.7 km) from India over the Indian Ocean towards the Maldives Islands. Regional effects probably dominate but are not strictly confined to the land area, and the effects will be driven by regional air circulation.

The largest reductions are found in the Northern Hemisphere mid-latitudes. The region of the spectrum of light radiation most affected seems to be the visible and infrared rather than the ultraviolet part of the spectrum.

Pan Evaporation Data

Over the last 50 or so years, pan evaporation has been carefully monitored. For decades, nobody took much notice of the pan evaporation measurements. But in the 1990s in Europe, Israel, and North America, scientists spotted something that at the time was considered very strange, the rate of evaporation was falling although they had expected it to increase due to global warming. The same trend has been observed in China over a similar period. A decrease in solar irradiance is cited to be the driving force. However, unlike in other areas of the world, in China the decrease in solar irradiance was not always accompanied by an increase in cloud cover and precipitation. It is believed that aerosols may play a critical role in the decrease of solar irradiance in China.

BBC Horizon producer David Sington believes that many climate scientists regard the pan-evaporation data as the most convincing evidence of solar dimming. Pan evaporation experiments are easy to reproduce with low-cost equipment, there are many pans used for agriculture all over the world and in many instances, and the data has been collected for nearly a half century. However, pan evaporation depends on some additional factors besides net radiation from the sun. The other two major factors are vapor pressure deficit and wind speed. The ambient temperature turns out to be a negligible factor. The pan evaporation data corroborates the data gathered by radiometer and fills in the gaps in the data obtained using pyranometers. With adjustments to these factors, pan evaporation data has been compared to results of climate simulations.

Probable Causes

The incomplete combustion of fossil fuels (such as diesel) and wood releases black carbon into the air. Though black carbon, most of which is soot, is an extremely small component of air pollution at land surface levels, the phenomenon has a significant heating effect on the atmosphere at altitudes above two kilometers (6,562 feet). Also, it dims the surface of the ocean by absorbing solar radiation.

Experiments in the Maldives (comparing the atmosphere over the northern and southern islands) in the 1990s showed that the effect of macroscopic pollutants in the atmosphere at that time (blown south from India) caused about a 10% reduction in sunlight reaching the surface in the area under the pollution cloud - a much greater reduction than expected from the presence of the particles themselves Prior to the research being undertaken, predictions were of a 0.5-1% effect from particulate matter; the variation from prediction may be explained by cloud formation with the particles acting as the focus for droplet creation. Clouds are very effective at reflecting light back out into space.

The phenomenon underlying global dimming may also have regional effects. While most of the earth has warmed, the regions that are downwind from major sources of air pollution (specifically sulfur dioxide emissions) have generally cooled. This may explain the cooling of the eastern United States relative to the warming western part.

Some climate scientists have theorized that aircraft contrails (also called vapor trails) are implicated in global dimming, but the constant flow of air traffic previously meant that this could not be tested. The near-total shutdown of civil air traffic during the three days following the September 11, 2001 attacks afforded a rare opportunity in which to observe the climate of the United States absent from the effect of contrails. During this period, an increase in diurnal temperature variation of over 1° C was observed in some parts of the U.S., i.e. aircraft contrails may have been raising nighttime temperatures and/or lowering daytime temperatures by much more than previously thought.

Airborne volcanic ash can reflect the Sun's rays back out into space and cool the planet. Dips in earth temperatures have been observed from large volcano eruptions such as Mount Agung in Bali that erupted in 1963, El Chichon (Mexico) 1983, Ruiz (Colombia) 1985, and Pinatubo (Philippines) 1991. But even for major eruptions, the ash clouds remain only for relatively short periods.

Recent reversal of the trend Wild *et al.*, using measurements over land report brightening since 1990. and Pinker *et al.*, found that slight dimming continued over land while brightening occurred over the ocean. Hence, over the land surface, Wild *et al.*, and Pinker *et al.*, disagree. A 2007 NASA sponsored satellite-based study sheds light on the puzzling observations by other scientists that the amount of sunlight reaching Earth's surface had been steadily declining in recent decades, suddenly started to rebound around 1990. This switch from a "global dimming" trend to a "brightening" trend happened just as global aerosol levels started to decline.

It is likely that at least some of this change, particularly over Europe, is due to decreases in pollution. Most governments of developed nations have done more to reduce aerosols released into the atmosphere, which helps reduce global dimming, than to reduce CO_2 emissions.

Sulfate aerosols have declined significantly since 1970 with the Clean Air Act in the United States and similar policies in Europe. The Clean Air Act was strengthened in 1977 and 1990. According to the EPA, from 1970 to 2005, total emissions of the six principal air pollutants, including PM's, dropped by 53 percent in the US. In 1975, the masked effects of trapped greenhouse gases finally started to emerge and have dominated ever since.

The Baseline Surface Radiation Network (BSRN) has been collecting surface measurements. BSRN was started in the early 1990s and updated the archives in this time. Analysis of recent data reveals that the surface of the planet has brightened by about 4% in the past decade. The brightening trend is corroborated by other data, including satellite analyses.

Relationship to Hydrological Cycle

Pollution produced by humans may be seriously weakening the Earth's water cycle - reducing rainfall and threatening fresh water supplies. A 2001 study by researchers at the Scripps Institution of Oceanography suggests that tiny particles of soot and other pollutants have a significant effect on the hydrological cycle. "The energy for the hydrological cycle comes from sunlight. As sunlight heats the ocean, water escapes into the atmosphere and falls out as rain. So as aerosols cut down sunlight by large amounts, they may be spinning down the hydrological cycle of the planet." according to prof. V. Ramanathan.

Large scale changes in weather patterns may also have been caused by global dimming. Climate models speculatively suggest that this reduction in sunshine at the surface may have led to the failure of the monsoon in sub-Saharan Africa during the 1970s and 1980s, together with the associated famines such as the Sahel drought, caused by Northern hemisphere pollution cooling the Atlantic. Because of this, the Tropical rain belt may not have risen to its northern latitudes, thus causing an absence of seasonal rains. This claim is not universally accepted and is very difficult to test.

It is also concluded that the imbalance between global dimming and global warming at the surface leads to weaker turbulent heat fluxes to the atmosphere. This means globally reduced evaporation and hence precipitation occur in a dimmer and warmer world, which could ultimately lead to a more humid atmosphere in which it rains less.

A natural form of large scale environmental shading/ dimming has been identified that affected the 2006 northern hemisphere hurricane season. The NASA study found that several major dust storms in June and July in the Sahara desert sent dust drifting over the Atlantic Ocean and through several effects caused cooling of the waters - and thus deadening the development of hurricanes.

Relationship to Global Warming

Some scientists now consider that the effects of global dimming have masked the effect of global warming to some extent and that resolving global dimming may therefore lead to increases in predictions of future temperature rise. According to Beate Liepert, "We lived in a global warming plus a global dimming world and now we are taking out global dimming. So we end up with the global warming world, which will be much worse than we thought it will be, much hotter." The magnitude of this masking effect is one of the central problems in climate change with significant implications for future climate changes and policy responses to global warming.

But it's much more complicated than an either warming or dimming issue. Global warming and global dimming are not mutually exclusive or contradictory. In a paper published

March 8, 2005 in the American Geophysical Union's Geophysical Research Letters, a research team led by Anastasia Romanou of Columbia University's Department of Applied Physics and Mathematics, New York, also showed that the apparently opposing forces of global warming and global dimming can occur at the same time. Global dimming interacts with global warming by blocking sunlight that would otherwise cause evaporation and the particulates bind to water droplets. Water vapor is one of the greenhouse gases. On the other hand, global dimming is affected by evaporation and rain. Rain has the effect of clearing out polluted skies.

Climatologists are stressing that the roots of both global dimming-causing pollutants and global warming-causing greenhouse gases have to be dealt with together and soon.

Possible use to mitigate Global Warming

Some scientists have suggested using aerosols to stave off the effects of global warming as an emergency measure. Russian expert Mikhail Budyko understood this relationship very early on. In 1974, he suggested that if global warming became a problem, we could cool down the planet by burning sulfur in the stratosphere, which would create a haze. According to Ramanathan (1988), an increase in planetary albedo of just 0.5 percent is sufficient to halve the effect of a CO_2 doubling.

However, we would still face many problems, such as:

- Using sulfates causes environmental problems such as acid rain
- Using carbon black causes human health problems
- Dimming causes ecological problems such as changes in evaporation and rainfall patterns
- Droughts and/or increased rainfall cause problems for agriculture
- Aerosol has a relatively short lifetime

"Ideas that we should increase aerosol emissions to counteract global warming have been described as a 'Faustian

"Ideas that we should increase aerosol emissions to counteract global warming have been described as a 'Faustian bargain' because that would imply an ever increasing amount of emissions in order to match the accumulated greenhouse gas in the atmosphere, with ever increasing monetary and health costs." In essence, the sources of both greenhouse gases and air particulates must be addressed.

Glossary

A

Abatement is the reduction or elimination of the degree or intensity of emissions i.e. pollution.

Abiotic Resources are the resources which are considered abiotic and therefore not renewable. Zinc ore and crude oil are examples of abiotic resources.

Acceptable Daily Intake is the highest daily amount of a substance that may be consumed over a lifetime without adverse effects.

Acid Deposition is a comprehensive term for the various ways acidic compounds precipitate from the atmosphere and deposit onto surfaces. It can include:

- wet deposition by means of acid rain, fog, and snow; and
- dry deposition of acidic particles (aerosols).

Acid Rain is rain mixed mainly with nitric and sulphuric acid, that arise from emissions released during the burning of fossil fuels.

Acute Exposure is one or a series of short-term exposures generally lasting less than 24 hours.

Adaptability refers to the degree to which adjustments are possible in practices, processes, or structures of systems to projected or actual changes of climate. Adaptation can be spontaneous or planned, and be carried out in response to or in anticipation of changes in conditions.

Aerobic composting is a method of composting organic waste using bacteria that need oxygen. This requires that the waste be exposed to air either by turning or by forcing air through pipes that pass through the material.

Aerosols are particles of solid or liquid matter that can remain suspended in air from a few minutes to many months depending on the particle size and weight.

Air is a mixture of gases containing about 78 percent nitrogen; 21 percent oxygen; less than 1 percent of carbon dioxide argon, and other gases; and varying amounts of water vapor.

Air Monitoring is the sampling for and measuring of pollutants present in the atmosphere.

Air Pollution is the degradation of air quality resulting from unwanted chemicals or other materials occurring in the air.

Air Pollutants are amounts of foreign and/or natural substances occurring in the atmosphere that may result in adverse effects to humans, animals, vegetation, and/or materials.

Air Quality Standard (AQS) is the prescribed level of a pollutant in the outside air that should not be exceeded during a specific time period to protect public health.

Alternative Fuel are fuels such as methanol, ethanol, natural gas, and liquid petroleum gas that are cleaner and help to meet mobile and stationary emission standards. These fuels may be used in place of less clean fuels for powering motor vehicles.

Ambient Air is the air occurring at a particular time and place outside of structures. Often used interchangeably with outdoor air.

Ambient Air Quality Standards (AAQS) are health and welfare-based standards for outdoor air which identify the maximum acceptable average concentrations of air pollutants during a specified period of time.

Ammonia is a pungent colorless gaseous compound of nitrogen and hydrogen that is very soluble in water and can easily be condensed into a liquid by cold and pressure.

Ammonia reacts with NOx to form ammonium nitrate — a major PM2.5 component in the Western United States.

Asbestos is a mineral fiber that can pollute air or water and cause cancer or asbestosis when inhaled. The U.S. EPA has banned or severely restricted its use in manufacturing and construction and the ARB has imposed limits on the amount of asbestos in serpentine rock that is used for surfacing applications.

Atmosphere is the gaseous mass or envelope of air surrounding the Earth. From ground-level up, the atmosphere is further subdivided into the troposphere, stratosphere, mesosphere, and the thermosphere.

Aquaculture, or pisceculture is the breeding or rearing of freshwater or marine fish in captivity, fish farming.

Index

❒ ❒ ❒ ❒ ❒